SKY WINGS

Part of the WINGS trilogy
*Tales of survival, magic and adventure, and of
wildlife in all its fascinating and true detail*

OTHER TITLES IN THE SERIES
On Silent Wings
Wild Wings

Reviews of the series:

'Puts Don Conroy's owls on an equal footing with
Richard Adams's rabbits (*Watership Down*)
and Tom McCaughren's foxes'
EVENING HERALD

'a welcome addition to the rank of
Irish novels for children'
CHILDREN'S BOOKS IN IRELAND

'Conroy's descriptive powers ensure immediate,
almost overwhelming images'
BOOKS IRELAND

DON CONROY

Well known from television for his expertise on wildlife, Don is also an artist, specialising in nature illustration and cartoons, and a storyteller. He has made a particular study of the barn owl. He has written many books.

OTHER BOOKS BY DON CONROY

The Celestial Child

THE WOODLAND FRIENDS SERIES
FOR YOUNG READERS

The Owl Who Couldn't Give a Hoot!
The Tiger Who Was a Roaring Success!
The Hedgehog's Prickly Problem!
The Bat Who Was All in a Flap!

LEARN TO DRAW

Cartoon Fun
Wildlife Fun

FOR ADULTS AND CHILDREN

Bird Life in Ireland
text: Jim Wilson, illustrations: Don Conroy

SKY WINGS

Don Conroy

THE O'BRIEN PRESS
DUBLIN

This revised and re-edited version first published 1995
by The O'Brien Press Ltd.,
20 Victoria Road, Rathgar, Dublin 6, Ireland.
Tel: +353 1 4923333; Fax: +353 1 4922777
E-mail books@obrien.ie
Website www.obrien.ie
First published 1992. Reprinted 2000.

ISBN 0-86278-419-0

British Library Cataloguing-in-Publication Data
Conroy, Don
Sky Wings
I. Title
823.914 [J]

2 3 4 5 6 7 8
00 01 02 03 04

The O'Brien Press receives
assistance from

The Arts Council
An Chomhairle Ealaíon

Colour separations: C&A Print Services Ltd.
Printing: Guernsey Press Ltd.

There is nothing more sacred in life than
what is most simple

John Millington Synge

DEDICATION
For my family and friends

CONTENTS

INVOCATION OF THE WORLD

Let us speak for the Earth
Sing for the Earth
Dance for the Earth
Soar for the Earth

Oh Sun, lend us your light and warmth
To sustain our life.
Oh Moon and Stars, guide us
Through the night with your pure light

Let our life blossom
Like the buds on the trees

Let us bear good fruit
Inspire us
Fill us with wisdom
May our brief flickering lives
Reflect your eternal song.

from *The Sacred Book of Ravens*

CHAPTER 1

Raven's View

Over the jade-green sea Sacer flapped her long pointed wings. There was still the bite of winter in the winds, chilling her body. Climbing high in the sky, her wild dark eyes watched a grey seal bob up from the green swell, then drop back again under the water. Up ahead, the evening sun burnished the cliffs with gold.

Wheeling and spinning, she passed over the knife-edged rocks. A colony of shags held their countenance as they dried their wings in the cold evening air. A dainty kittiwake moved gently over the surging waves. Sacer glanced from on high at the passing gull but, despite hunger pangs, the oily flavour of gull didn't tempt the peregrine. She had tasted it once as a chick and hadn't liked it.

As she approached the cliffs, feelings of joy and sorrow mingled in her mind. She remembered the comfort of the eyrie as she sat with her sister and brother waiting for their parents to return with food; the tugging games she played with them over a pigeon bone; the jostling for position on the ledge. Her sister always won because she was the eldest and the strongest.

It seemed such a long time since the eyrie was active and lively with the flapping, preening and exploring of the young falcons. Sacer recalled how her mother would chase away the great black-backed gulls when they came too close to the nest. Then she withdrew into troubled thoughts, remembering the day the two Nusham had climbed down the sheer cliffs and taken her brother and sister away in a bag; her mother screaming, watching helplessly as the Nusham plucked her young away from her; her father, the tiercel, swooping bravely at the Nusham, but to no avail.

One of the Nusham had wanted to take Sacer too.

'She's too young,' the other had said. 'Leave her. They only end up as screamers if you take them too early. We'd better get out of here. Looks like a storm brewing.'

Sacer recalled how the ravens of the Sacred Cliffs had come the next day and sat with her parents for a long time.

Night had already descended as Sacer moved along the dizzying cliffs. It seemed to her that the stars were near enough to fly to. The air was clear and cold and, from the stillness, eyes marked her passing. She gazed down to where the eyrie was and passed over it slowly, alighting nearby and folding her dark brown wings that nature would colour grey some day, like her parents' plumage.

She preened at her deep cream breast feathers, shifted on her yellow legs, then stretched luxuriously, checked a dishevelled tail feather with her bill and placed it back in position. She watched the foaming waves below as she perched motionless but alert on a ledge, surveying the surrounding seascape.

In her mind's eye Sacer could see herself flying in unison with her parents, exploring every crevice of the cliffs – the noisy kittiwakes, the razorbills, the guillemots and the stiff-winged fulmars that shared the cliffs, nesting there. Choughs, ravens, jackdaws and doves had also nested on the sheer cliffs. A colony of shags used a sheltered corner of a sea stack to build their untidy nests. The cliffs had been alive with squawking, wailing and screaming. Sacer knew that once the breeding season came again the cliffs would once more echo with the loud clamour of the nesting colonies.

The wind raged, showing no sign of abating. Glancing over at the empty nest, Sacer remembered

Granet, the old raven, arriving one evening from the Sacred Cliffs, explaining to her about the mysterious death of her parents. As she looked into his moist eyes he whispered to the sea: 'The wind has gone with my friends.'

There was a deep sadness in his eyes as he advised her to fly to the lowlands and hunt by the estuaries. 'There you'll have a chance to survive the harsh winter,' he added.

Well, Sacer had taken his advice and had made it through the first winter alone. She was glad to be back, but she wondered what she would do now. She

14

was aware that she was changing. Her powers of perception and observation were growing rapidly and life revealed new mysteries each day. Sacer shifted over to a crevice in the rocks so that she could sleep soundly away from the winds.

CHAPTER 2

Moving Out

The herring gulls clouded over the city dump. It was the day the dustbin trucks delivered tons of edible refuse from hotels, restaurants, cafés and private houses. Starlings and jackdaws joined in the orgy of eating. The gulls followed the bulldozer as it spread the refuse. Another bulldozer was busy levelling and burning the offal. The rain earlier had helped to keep the putrid smells down. Not that it bothered the birds – their sense of smell was poor.

Hack, the one-eyed rat, sniffed the many smells that wafted upwards towards the entrance to their lair. Anxiously he waited with his comrades for dusk to come, when they could feast and gorge on all those delicious morsels. Yet one thing bothered him. It seemed that each day the bulldozers were getting nearer and nearer to the lair, which had remained undisturbed for such a long time. The last major disturbance had killed many of his comrades, and had also caused a cave-in. It had taken several days to clear the mess and make the lair habitable again.

'Stay here,' Hack ordered the others, as he moved quietly over plastic bags and empty cans.

He climbed up on to some debris and scanned the area. The Nusham were too busy to notice him, but he was spotted from a pylon.

A hungry female kestrel bobbed in excitement, then lifted off from the wires and headed in for the kill. While she was making her silent attack, a hooded crow sitting on a parked truck raised his wings and flapped rapidly towards her. Calling harshly, the hooded crow dived at the kestrel. He was soon joined by several rooks and magpies. Together they harried and tormented the kestrel through several fields, until she finally out-manoeuvred them and sped away to safety.

Hack cowered under an old chair watching the whole episode. When the hooded crow flew back, Hack recognised him. It was Whizzer. The rat squealed a greeting. The crow looked surprised and flew down to greet him.

'Well, we meet again,' said Whizzer. 'It's been a long time!'

Hack moved closer. 'Thank you, dear comrade, for

defending me from that damned kestrel,' he said.

The hooded crow had no idea that the kestrel had been on her way to attack the rat. He liked to hassle kestrels, especially if they had just caught a fresh meal, as they would be forced to discard it after several dive bombs and sharp pecks on the back.

'Come and dine with us,' offered Hack. 'I'd like you to meet our new leader.'

The crow recoiled.

'Don't worry,' sniggered Hack. 'He's nothing like Fericul or Natas. Of course, you never met Prince Natas ... just as well.'

Hack moved to the entrance, squealed his arrival, then scurried underground. The crow looked in cautiously.

'Come on in to our inner sanctum,' said a voice from behind.

Whizzer looked around and there stood another rat he recognised. It was Spike.

'After you!' said the rat.

The crow crouched and went underground. Ahead of him he could see many rats scurrying about. 'I hope you weren't seen,' said a voice from behind a long pipe. 'We don't want to arouse unwelcome attention.'

The crow looked around nervously. Furry bodies came from various chambers and sat on their haunches, twitching their whiskers and staring at Whizzer.

'You're safe here,' said Hack reassuringly. 'Allow me to introduce you to our great leader.'

From the shadows came a white albino rat, slightly larger than the brown rats.

'This is General Spook.'

The crow sensed no threat from the unusual rodent.

'This is Whizzer,' said Hack, 'an old comrade to the Emperor Fericul.'

'Before my time,' remarked Spook with a snigger.

'My feathered friend here has just saved my hide from a kestrel attack,' Hack continued. The other rats cheered loudly.

'Well done, comrade!' they squealed in chorus.

Several rats entered, carrying food. Whizzer's eyes gleamed.

'Are you hungry?' asked Spook. 'Join us for dinner.'

They gorged on chicken legs, bacon, sausages and bread. After they had eaten their fill they regaled each other with tales of the Emperor Fericul and Prince Natas. Then Whizzer warned them about the bulldozers.

'They'll be digging and levelling here soon, tomorrow or the next day.'

The rats became very anxious. The fear of the dreaded diggers tearing apart their homes shattered any hopes of staying around the dump, and they knew it would be just a matter of time before they'd have to move. Most of them remembered their kin being destroyed or mutilated by the machines.

Spook agreed that it was becoming dangerous to stay.

'Why don't you live in Ratland?' asked Whizzer. 'You'd be a lot safer there.'

Spook twitched his whiskers and tugged nervously at his tail. 'What do you think?' he asked, looking at Spike and Hack.

'Well, it is our ancient kingdom, even if it does give me the creeps,' Hack remarked.

'No bulldozers or anything to bother us there,' said Spike. 'I think a small group of us should go, even for a few weeks, to see if we like it. Twenty would be enough for a start.'

'What's the weather like?' asked Spook.

'Cold, but dry,' replied Hack.

Okay, that settles it, thought Spook. We'll go to-night. 'What about you, Whizzer? Would you like to join us?'

'Why not!' said the crow. 'I've become something of an outcast since my run-in with the ravens of the Sacred Cliffs.'

*   *   *

The road was bright, patterned with inky shadows cast from the trees that lined the route.

'Keep a sharp lookout. We don't want to be supper for any owl,' whispered Spook.

Hack and Spike were glad that Spook had become leader. He was very cunning, and avoided trouble for the most part, unlike the Emperor Fericul who was cold and brutal, and Prince Natas who was sly, devious and just as dangerous. Spook seemed to get on with the mice and shrews. They trusted him and he always gave them good advice.

As the little group moved through the comforting darkness there was no sign of the Nusham or their deadly cars that flashed such dazzling lights. After some time they left the silent road and moved under a fence and across a field. Cattle stood huddled together beside a hedgerow, sleeping. The fields were bathed in silvery light. The rats stopped to rest, sniffed the cold air, and sat on their humped hindquarters. Spook bristled his fur, then, snout twitching, he whispered: 'I smell the sweet odour of bird. Hack, take six of our strongest comrades and find us some supper.'

'No sooner said than done,' grinned Hack.

The rats moved silently away through the long grasses. A vixen screamed in the distance, shattering the silence of the night. The rats stopped in their tracks and huddled in fear, snouts and whiskers twitching nervously.

'It's all right,' insisted Hack. 'It's too far away for us to be concerned about. Now, come on!'

A female pheasant slept in her lightly-lined nest,

near the hedgerow, her warm body brooding fourteen brown eggs. She was unaware that, in the silence, brown bristling beasts were moving in for the kill.

Suddenly they leapt from the long grasses. Jagged incisors sank into her neck, clawed feet scurried over her body. In a panic the pheasant hissed and twisted herself, breaking several eggs, but the rats would not release their grip. She kicked vainly, twitched spasmodically, then fell silently in a heap.

They squealed their high-pitched squeals of triumph, which signalled the others to hurry and join them. Spook looked pleased.

'Let's hear it for the advance party!' The other rats squealed and waved their tails in praise.

'Did I mention *party*?' Spook sniggered.

'Let's eat,' said Spike.

They gorged on warm pheasant and lapped up the contents of the eggs, then they lay around like bloated leeches.

* * *

The next morning found the male pheasant frantically circling the broken eggs, and the creamy mottled feathers all strewn about.

CHAPTER 3

Guardians of
the Sacred Cliffs

In the soft light of early dawn a raven slipped quietly across the sky like a shadow.

A strong coconut fragrance hung in the air from the gorse bushes near the cliffs. The clear warbling sound of a skylark could be heard as he fluttered in the air, proclaiming his territory. Below, his mate incubated her four olive-brown speckled white eggs. These were the first of two or three broods she planned to have during the breeding season.

A cock stonechat perched upright on a gorse branch carrying a beakful of insect larvae, then flew down to the base of the bush where his mate sat in her moss-lined nest with her newly-hatched clutch of five.

Sacer sat, high up on a ledge, warming herself in the morning sun. Looking at the empty eyrie, she remembered how her mother would advise her that meticulous care and attention must be given to one's feathers.

'A clean bird is a healthy bird!' she would say.

Sacer had been back on the cliffs several days now. It felt good, but a little lonely. She watched the herring gulls hang in the sky in the updraughts. Fulmars gabbled as they planed around the cove.

In the distance the Sacred Cliffs seemed shrouded in a soft diffusion of mist and light. Sacer wanted so much to explore them, but she knew it was out of bounds. Her parents had spent a great deal of time there and when she or her family enquired about the Sacred Cliffs her father always said he would tell them when the time was right. He never did.

She watched a grey seal move through the shimmering water, then pull its sleek frame on to the rocks below. Cormorants sat statue-like on the shiny rocks. Sacer felt hungry. She had caught a woodpigeon in the fields several days ago, but had had to abandon it after being mobbed by six hooded crows. They in turn had pulled it apart and gulped down most of it. The rest of it was pinched by a hungry stoat. Since then Sacer had only managed to catch a meadow pipit.

Lifting her wings, she launched herself into the sky. Climbing higher, wheeling and spinning, she rode the warm air. She could see the bright green and soft brown of the fields merging and blending with the rough ground where the heather and gorse grew. Spiralling higher, up and up, she soared above the cliffs.

Two ravens followed her at a discreet distance.

The cliffs were loud with the clamour of seabirds. Choughs up ahead floated and skirted along the cliffs. Their rising and falling flight was in perfect unison. Soon they disappeared behind a ridge.

Spiralling downwards now, Sacer alighted on a lichen-covered rock that was dressed with delicate sea-pink flowers. She knew every dip and fold of this stretch of the cliffs; it was her ancestral home and she was proud of that. The sun made her blink. She closed her eyes to slits, and looked out to sea. It appeared calm and peaceful now, but could just as quickly turn into a savage tide leaping in anger, with its white waves heaving and tossing at the base of the cliffs.

Then she noticed a flock of pigeons, moving at cliff height across the sea. Their rapid wingbeat was bringing them purposefully towards land. Sacer pulled herself into instant alertness, slipped off the ledge and darted in pursuit. The pigeons sensed danger and turned along the side of the cliff. One had separated from the others and flapped on panicked wings. Yet Sacer could not catch it; the racing pigeon was swifter than the falcon. The pigeon re-joined the others and they circled in unison, sensing that danger had passed.

But Sacer had not given up. She climbed vertically into the sky, then levelling out she pulled her wings close to her body and dived at terrific speed, bullet-like through the air, taking a pigeon completely by surprise. Talons raked its breast. A cloud of feathers exploded into the air as the racer was torn from the sky. The other pigeons sped away without looking back.

A cry of alarm came from an oystercatcher, which flew out to sea, scolding loudly.

The peregrine flapped over to a ledge, mantled her kill and held it firm in her yellow feet. For generations her kind had survived in this harsh and hostile environment by being powerful hunters. Bobbing and bowing, eyes ever watchful, Sacer checked to see if any gull or crow was waiting to ambush her and take her hard-earned meal. All seemed quiet. She immediately began to pluck the breast feathers, then tear succulent slivers of flesh from the plump breast of the pigeon.

Sacer ate the meat to the bone, until only the wings and legs remained. As she crouched with full crop she noticed a shining band around one of the pigeon's legs, but she thought no more of it. The sun blazed from the cloudless sky.

Sacer sat and rested on a nearby ledge. She felt lethargic and her eyelids began to droop. Suddenly she was fully alert as heavy, broad-shadowed wings passed overhead and two ravens swooped down to stand alongside her. One stared hard at her, while the other pulled at the dead pigeon's leg.

'You have killed a racer, one of the Nusham's birds,' said the latter, in shocked tones.

Sacer remained still and silent.

'We are the guardians of the Sacred Cliffs,' said the other raven.

'By doing this you have invited trouble on us. The Nusham will come with the death guns.'

'You'd better follow us,' said the first raven. Sacer felt she didn't have much choice.

They opened their wings and lifted off into the air, one on either side of Sacer, leading her to the Sacred Cliffs. They passed through the vibrant sunlight in silence, Sacer looking back with longing at the cliffs that had once been her home.

Up ahead more cliffs climbed skywards. The rocks stood tall, like stone monuments carved by ancient earth spirits. As they moved through the mysterious mist Sacer could see the massive ringed rocks that circled the plateau. One raven croaked loudly to sound their arrival.

CHAPTER 4

Strange Dreams

The night was warm and still. The silver moon hung like a pearl in the starry sky. Crag set out on his nightly search for food. Padding along the hedgerow, he stopped to sniff the air – this was how he kept himself well-informed of his surroundings. There was a smell of Nusham, but it was faint. He could also smell mice and rats and there was a strong smell of rabbit nearby. He circled around, in and out of the dark shadows cast by the hedgerow. A rotten tree stump, partially covered with wood sorrel, revealed some insect larvae which he promptly licked up. Suddenly, from a clump of stinging and white-dead nettles a hedgehog emerged. 'I was after them,' he scolded.

The fox jerked a little, startled.

'Well, that's a good one!' said Hotchiwichi. 'I've finally managed to sneak up on you.'

'Night peace, old friend. How are you?' asked Crag.

'Oh, very well. I feel fresh and invigorated after my long sleep. You should try it sometime – oh, of course ... you can't. Silly me. Have things been good with you?' the hedgehog enquired.

'Quiet and peaceful. The way I like it. I somehow managed to survive the hunts, the guns and the traps for another season, thank heavens.' Crag yawned and scratched behind his ear, then, pulling at the decaying stump, he revealed more juicy larvae.

'Help yourself!' said the fox.

'Don't mind if I do.' Hotchiwichi polished off the grubs.

Crag nosed the air, then padded over to the fence which led into a narrow road. The hedgehog followed behind. Crag checked for car lights; all was clear so he trotted over to a dead rabbit, hit earlier by a car. He sniffed it gingerly, then began to feed.

'A fox need hardly ever hunt during these months,' he mused. 'The Nusham kill more wild creatures this way than they do with their traps.'

'Who're you telling?' retorted the hedgehog. 'I've lost nearly all my relatives this way.'

The fox felt a bit guilty, eating in front of Hotchiwichi.

'Oh, it's all right,' said the hedgehog. 'No point in

letting it go to waste. It'd only be eaten by the rats and magpies later.' He moved over to the verge and, plucking a slug from the long grass, gulped it down quickly. 'I prefer snails really, but when a slug is on offer I can't refuse.'

Crag ate his fill, then moved off towards the other fields.

'Wait for me,' said Hotchiwichi as he trundled along.

They headed for the river, where they sat under the starlit sky, watching the quiet babbling water meander through the meadows. Crag slipped down to drink from the cool water.

'This feels good,' he murmured as he stretched his body. Then he padded along the muddy bank, Hotchiwichi still trundling behind. Crag crouched beside an alder tree which cast long shadows over the sparkling water.

'Suppose you wanted to eat me,' said Hotchiwichi, 'which of course I know you wouldn't ... '

'Well, not after that feed of rabbit,' smiled Crag.

The hedgehog chuckled. 'What I'm trying to say is, we hedgehogs are clever, really. At the first sign of danger we can roll into a ball and be completely protected by our spiky armour. How many creatures could boast of that? Hey, Crag? Well?'

'Oh, it's true. A very useful technique,' said the fox. 'Almost foolproof.'

'What do you mean by that?' asked the hedgehog.

'Well, Hotchi, if you weren't the old friend which you are, and if I were really hungry and came across a tasty hedgehog all curled up ...'

'Yes? What would you do, Crag? Nothing! You must admit I have you there!' retorted the hedgehog gleefully.

'Well, I'd simply roll you down into the water, Hotchi. Soon you'd uncurl, then I'd–'

'Okay, old pal,' said Hotchi. 'No wonder they call you crafty. You don't miss a trick.'

'I can't afford to,' replied Crag.

They sat silently, watching the movement of the water.

'I wonder how many of our kind have sat and watched here?' mused Hotchi.

'I followed the river once! It journeys all the way to the sea,' declared Crag.

'It's a bit like life,' said Hotchi. 'We're all heading back to the eternal seas.'

'True,' Crag agreed. 'Nothing stands still.' He was about to go on with more deep thoughts, but just then Bawson the badger passed through the clearing. He shuffled over the scrubby bank to them.

'Night peace, dear friends,' said the badger.

Crag and Hotchiwichi greeted him warmly. A branch suddenly floated by on the river, startling Bawson. The badger looked up anxiously at the bright moon, then gave a shudder of fear.

'Is everything all right, dear friend?' asked Crag.

'Well, yes and no,' replied Bawson.

Then he spoke slowly, fixing his gaze beyond them. 'I've been having bad dreams again. We're in a mysterious place ... strange dark forms can be seen ... crumbling walls with skulls and bones everywhere ... a thick green fog seeps through the passages and spills over the land ... there's something hidden, lurking in this weird fog as it twists into hideous forms. There are rats everywhere ... fear, horror and death follow in the wake of this slimy green fog.'

'You're giving me the creeps,' said Hotchi.

'Perhaps you're still remembering that time when you had to journey down to Ratland,' said the old fox. 'Of course, we're rid of the rat problem now, so you shouldn't trouble yourself any more with those night-mares.'

'I had another bad dream,' sighed the

badger. 'The Nusham were near the sett ...' Bawson began to tremble all over.

'Take it easy, old friend. Try and put these thoughts out of your mind. Look around you. It's a lovely peaceful night. Let's just enjoy it.'

Suddenly a loud shriek startled the three of them, and a barn owl swooped down.

'Night peace,' said Kos.

'Night peace is right! You nearly scared us to death. If I live till I'm sixty I'll never get used to your shriek,' said Hotchiwichi. This brought a loud laugh of relief from the badger.

'Would you like to hear my good news?' asked the barn owl. They all nodded.

'Crannóg has laid four eggs. I've caught five rats already tonight for our secret larder. There seem to be a lot of rodents about these evenings.'

With that Bawson became fretful again.

CHAPTER 5

The Lesson

Sacer sat on a ledge in silence, listening to the wind. She had set her gaze on the horizon, watching in the distance the guillemots and razorbills flying out to sea, returning with food for their young and then heading out again. This activity continued all day. The ravens had fed her, but little had been said. She wondered what was in store for her here on these Sacred Cliffs.

There was a sudden rush of wings – and as she turned her head to face the sound Sacer could see a large gathering of ravens coming in over the hills. They alighted on the plateau amid deep-throated calls. Then, settling, they each took up different positions on the rocks and sat like sentinels. An old raven came flapping over and sat staring at the peregrine.

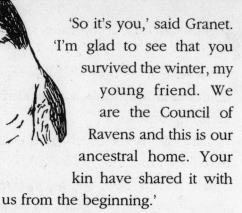

'So it's you,' said Granet. 'I'm glad to see that you survived the winter, my young friend. We are the Council of Ravens and this is our ancestral home. Your kin have shared it with us from the beginning.'

Sacer shifted nervously on her yellow legs but said nothing.

'As you know, I was a close friend of your parents,' Granet went on. 'They were dear to us all. Their strength and courage were unequalled. We deeply regret their untimely end.' His eyes clouded over in the sunlight. 'Their names are carved in the cave where we house the Sacred Feather and the *Sacred Book of Ravens.*'

The young peregrine knew nothing of these things but was relieved to find that the ravens were not hostile and she felt a great sense of pride at the words of the old raven.

'You're like your mother, a strong and powerful hunter. We've seen that. But you've killed a Nusham's prized pigeon. They won't take that lightly. Soon they'll come to the lower cliffs and look for you with the death guns. The Nusham may lose many birds through accident and carelessness, but they will not tolerate falcons taking any of their pigeons. In future you must hunt the woodpigeons, feral pigeons or rock doves ... '

Sacer realised now that this indeed was a serious matter and she looked anxiously towards the old raven for guidance.

'Don't worry too much,' said Granet. 'You may stay here for a time. This place will be a safe haven. Then you must go back to the lowlands. If you prove yourself worthy you may return to the Sacred Cliffs and take your rightful place as a guardian of this hallowed place. But for now you must learn the secret ways. We'll talk later, but I must rest now.'

* * *

Sacer sat in calm solitude and watched the early stars appear in the evening sky. The desolate cry of the curlew brought back memories of the winter estuaries where these waders sat in large flocks, huddled together for protection from the winter winds. She recalled how they and the redshanks would warn of her arrival over the grey skies, how they would explode into flight, circle for a time, then land again. The young falcon would then have to search elsewhere for a meal, running the gauntlet of attack from hooded crows, magpies and rooks.

But now her trail of memory was broken by a hefty raven who moved in swaggering gait towards her.

'Follow me,' he said in commanding tones.

He led her towards the entrance to a cave which was carefully concealed by gorse and heather. Sacer was watched closely by night-seeing eyes.

'Enter,' said Granet, from where he stood with the Council.

'You're welcome,' said Corvus, one of the elders, as Sacer moved cautiously towards them.

She could hear other ravens muttering quietly to themselves. Beyond the ravens in another passage a beautiful light arched across the cave. There was an air of mystery about the place which Sacer had never experienced before. The soft gentle rainbow light seemed to spill out, bathing everything in its radiance. The ravens watched Sacer's eyes. She seemed mesmerised.

'Would you like to see where this light comes from?' asked Granet.

Sacer jerked her head as if snapping out of a trance and nodded.

'Very well. Follow me,' he ordered.

As Granet moved into the other passage he seemed to be absorbed into the enchanting light. Corvus indicated to Sacer that she should enter. Trembling, she followed the old raven.

'This is the Sacred Feather, our most treasured possession, left to us by the Eagle of Light,' said Granet.

Sacer's eyes feasted on the precious object whose

warm glow bathed her with a beautiful sense of peace and serenity. It was like the feeling she got when her mother would nestle her warm body over her – that special feeling of security, of being completely protected from all dangers.

'This feather holds a special magic, which we may only use for the good of the planet,' Granet continued. 'If it is used for anything else, great destruction could befall us all. There have been attempts by the rodents to steal it but luckily they failed, thanks to the courage of our friends in the lowlands and the Eagles of Mount Eagle. It was while protecting these holy cliffs that your dear parents lost their lives.'

The peregrine continued to stare at the sacred object which seemed to illuminate the room.

'With this Feather our consciousness embraces infinity,' whispered Corvus. 'You are now being awakened to realities beyond nature's wondrous works. This Feather has enlightened, healed and aided us in so many ways, adding to the world's treasure of knowledge. Life is incomplete if all we seek is food, shelter and breeding. You must enhance yourself with knowledge, Sacer. Your quest must be for eternal wisdom.'

'There's a lot to learn,' Granet said warmly. 'Knowledge opens our minds to the sunlight of truth. And now, there's something else we wish to show you.'

They moved into another chamber which housed

a large rock with ornate carving on it. The top of the rock was flat and smooth, and sitting on it was a large book. The cover was beautifully studded with precious stones encased in gold, and a mysterious glow came from it also. Granet moved over to it and carefully flicked the cover with his bill. Sacer marvelled at the strange markings on the pages.

'This book was written by the Ancient Ones,' said Granet. 'It is the *Sacred Book of Ravens*, inspired by the Eagle of Light. Those pages contain all the secret wisdom and mysteries of life, dating back to before the coming of the Nusham. All we need to know is in its wondrous pages.

'The ravens of these cliffs have always possessed the gifts of the scribe and the reader. In recent times some others have mastered these skills. We wish to share this knowledge; no longer is wisdom for the privileged few.' Granet spoke solemnly.

'Not that all will embrace this wisdom,' added Corvus. 'Each one may choose to accept or reject. They make this choice and then they reap either the joys or sorrows of their decision.'

Sacer was spell-bound. She had never imagined such wonders. She caught a glimpse of the future, a future full of knowledge, goodness, wisdom ...

'It's time now to eat and rest,' Granet interrupted her thoughts. 'We'll talk again at first light ...'

*   *   *

Two men walked down from the cliffs, one carrying a shotgun, the other a rifle.

'No sign of that falcon,' said one of them. 'But we'll get it. Sooner or later I'll plug that damned bird.'

CHAPTER 6

Night of the Rodents

As the last rays of sun departed from the sky, the hordes of furry creatures knew that freedom of movement would once again be theirs. Squatting and twitching outside their lairs, the rats waited anxiously for the signal to move. Most of them had slept during the hours of daylight in their underground tunnels, safe from the dangerous eyes of their enemies – Nusham, foxes, stoats, mink, badgers, falcons and owls. But at night they must be vigilant; their enemies would be abroad hunting for them. Just as the moon appeared in the sky the rats could hear high-pitched squeals carried on the chilly night air, inviting them to a very important celebration and banquet in their ancient kingdom of Ratland. The rodents had been waiting for this occasion ever since they had heard the news on the night of the last full moon. All were invited.

Rats, shrews, mice and voles scurried through the darkness, sniffing the night air, their bristling furred bodies moving in frenzied excitement and expectation. Squealing their high-pitched squeals, eyes wide and alert, they poured out into the fields from their various hiding places, all bound for Ratland.

After their long journey they arrived at the massive rocks which stood like sentinels in front of the entrance. The place seemed dark and dreary as they entered the cold cobweb-covered corridors. They passed along the damp slimy passages, wondering was anyone there. It all seemed so quiet. As they entered the lower chambers their fear increased. The tunnel walls were made of dark glowering skulls. Empty shadowed sockets seemed to throw suspicious glances at any passerby.

Their frightened eyes stared ahead as they travelled down the silent passageways. Then suddenly, echoing through the chambers, the sound of laughter and gaiety could be plainly discerned. Rodents gaily flowed in and out of the chambers, greeting the new arrivals. More rodents lay around, warming themselves before a blazing fire, and feasting on the many different foods that Hack and the city rats had managed to find.

Spook sat proudly in the chair which had once

accommodated the feared Emperor Fericul and Prince Natas. Some of the rodents had never seen a white rat before and held him in awe. The fire flamed yellow and crimson and a group of female rats danced to a rodent melody, sung by a pack of shrews. The dancers encircled the fire, their bodies moving in unison like brown dancing flames. The rat-kings performed next and the merriment and laughter grew louder. The rat-kings had been born connected to each other by a strange knot in their tails. The others marvelled at this. Many rats believed it brought luck to have them in a colony.

Hack and Spike tossed another log on to the fire and the flames leapt higher. There was loud cheering and laughter as four buck rats sang a death chant to their enemies. Eyes were gleaming bright with yellow reflections from the fire and they all joined in the chorus, their squeals and screams piercing the chamber.

Then Hack called for silence. The crowds watched as he and Spike carefully placed a crown on Spook's head. Loud cheers and stamping of clawed feet were followed by a wild waving of tails. Spook stood proudly and accepted the crown and title of King Rat. A far cry from the cage he was reared in by the Nusham, he thought to himself.

'Speech! Speech! Speech!' The crowds yelled.

Spook bowed low to all sides of the chamber, then

moved over to the ancient carved stone and touched it reverently.

Turning to the crowd, he spoke: 'You do me a great honour. I am proud to accept this crown. I don't say I deserve it but I'll try to serve my comrades, or should I say, my subjects, to the best of my ability.'

There were loud cheers from all the rodents.

'It's nice to feel we're safe in this labyrinthine home of our ancient folk.'

More loud cheers from the spectators.

Spook continued, holding himself in a regal manner: 'The rodent is wise in the ways of the night. Our origins may be lost in the mists of time; those long-forgotten tribes who travelled throughout the world, establishing colonies and kingdoms; they may be gone but we have their homeland now.'

More loud cheers came from the rodents.

'We've retained the ancient language and the old ways but we've also embraced the new. That is important.

'We've experienced dangers too terrible to mention; we've suffered many catastrophes; we've had to leave our native homes. Monumental hatred has been heaped upon us by the Nusham. They class us as undesirables. We have been imprisoned, tortured and slain. But we rise again and will continue to do so until we're the dominant species on this planet!'

The whistles and squeals of approval left Hack and

Spike under no illusion that Spook was the most popular leader to date. They each whispered congratulations to him as he returned to his throne.

'Now! After such a powerful speech I think our King should feast,' Hack shouted. More food was brought in from the nearby chambers.

The rodents indulged in their own particular kind of feasting all night, finally dropping off to sleep. Replete, their hunger appeased, they lay bloated on the chamber floor. Spook sat drowsing on his throne, Hack and Spike sleeping on either side of him.

Suddenly, through drooping eyelids, Spook became aware of a pale green fog seeping in from one of the chambers. A chill of fear gripped him as he watched it sliding sluggishly along the walls. Shaking Hack and Spike awake, he pointed to the mysterious cloud at the entrance. The three of them moved slowly, climbing over the sleeping rodents, past the fire which was burning low. They moved cautiously into the green fog.

Suddenly they could see, crouched in the darkness, the large black form of a rat. It opened its eyes, which flamed red and glowed menacingly through the darkness. They stood terrified, then as quickly as the green fog had appeared it vanished, along with the phantom rat ...

CHAPTER 7

The Legacy

Spook commanded Hack and Spike to say nothing about the strange green fog. The following day they had pondered long and hard on what it could be. They wondered if it were wise to remain in Ratland. That night they moved away from the main chambers to talk in secret and decide what was best to do. Most of the rodents were out foraging for food, and on raiding parties to farms for eggs and grain, and would not be back until first light.

Hack scratched, and stretched. 'Well, maybe it was some trick of light,' he said. 'There's some green slime on the walls. Maybe when the walls became heated it threw off this green hue ...'

'Perhaps you're right,' said Spook. 'But how do you

explain the rat with the red glowing eyes? What do you think, Spike?'

Spike was about to reply when they saw a long shadow appear across the entrance, followed by a strange flapping. Their bodies went rigid with fear.

Suppressing a scream, Spook asked in a quivering voice: 'Who's there?'

'It's only me,' said Whizzer, the hooded crow.

The rats heaved a great sigh of relief and greeted him.

'I'm covered with cobwebs and slime.' Whizzer began to preen carefully. 'It's sure a long way down here.'

'Any news?' asked Spike.

'Nothing really to report, except I hear there's a new falcon on the Sacred Cliffs and she's being trained by the ravens.'

'Doesn't bother us,' stated Hack. 'We've dealt with falcons before.'

'Well, we don't need to concern ourselves with her,' added Whizzer. 'I've heard from reliable sources that she killed one of the Nusham racing pigeons, and they've been out searching for her with the death guns.'

'Now, isn't it grand that we have the Nusham doing our dirty work,' said Spook with a smirk.

'Er ... there is one thing ... what's that green fog in the chamber opposite?' enquired the hooded crow.

The rats trembled. 'Look!' yelled Spike. 'It's back!'

Quickly they scurried behind a rock as the green fog began to fill the chamber.

'What on earth is it?' asked Whizzer.

They could see the obscene blob form inside the clinging fog, then shape itself into a rat. It brought with it an air of brooding menace. The rats wondered if they should try and make a run for it, yet the green fog clung everywhere.

'Don't alarm yourselves!' said a deep throated voice. 'I mean you no harm, I've come to help you.'

The green fog began to evaporate, revealing a large black rat with blood-red eyes. The rats and the bird quaked, not knowing whether it was some loathsome spectre possessed of strange powers, or a full-blooded rat, not unlike Fericul or Natas.

Shivering, Hack braved a few words: 'This is our King Rat. May we be so bold as to enquire who you are and where you come from?'

The stranger stared hard at the others: 'I am Laab, Lord of the Underworld. This is my abode. I've delved into the secrets of magic, the forbidden fields of understanding. Come, I'll let you meet my army of fiends. I'll give you the power to destroy your enemies. Follow me!' said Lord Laab.

Terror-stricken, the three rats and Whizzer found themselves following the green fog down secret corridors, which they hadn't known existed.

The silence of death was all around as they passed along strange stone walls with ancient carvings, which seemed to possess deep dark secrets of the past. The mysterious rat entered a chamber and carefully circled a table of stone. There was something on the table, from which a strange light seemed to emanate and hover in clouds above.

'Enter!' commanded Lord Laab.

Spike, Spook, Hack and Whizzer glanced quickly at each other, hesitated briefly, then entered. They sensed a cold, unnatural chill. As they stood silently watching, Lord Laab reached into the clouds of smoke which were bellowing up from the table and very carefully took hold of something. They watched his eyes as he gazed with an evil look at the object which he was proudly holding.

'This, my friends, is what will give you the power you need to do the will of the Lords of the Underworld.'

Laab held it out. The others quaked at the sight.

'Fear not, dear friends, for this is the Claw of Darkness.' The very name sent shudders through them. 'I've brought it all the way from the underworld,' he said, indicating a passageway where two carved rodent statues were guarding the entrance, casting dark discomforting shadows along the ground.

'Don't alarm yourselves,' he continued, 'you don't

have to go down there. No one enters there and comes back ... *alive*!' He laughed loudly, the demonic sound echoing around the chambers.

He turned quickly to Spook: 'You're a King. Act like one! Take this!'

With trembling hands Spook accepted the Claw of Darkness. For a moment they all gazed at its sinister form.

'The birds have their Sacred Feather, which they can only use for good. There are no such restrictions on you,' he said slyly. 'You may do as you will. Now, leave, but make sure it doesn't fall into the wrong hands. I'll return again soon!'

The rats and the crow backed away, tripping over each other as they left. Spook, with a strained grasp on the Claw scurried out, stumbling over the others. Terrified to look back, they hurried to the safety of their chambers. When they reached the throne room Spook warned his companions to keep the whole thing a secret. Then, breaking into a nervous laugh, he added: 'Soon we'll try out our mysterious gift. Maybe I'll be a King with real power!'

CHAPTER 8

The Nomad

Sacer sat preening, using her talons for the facial feathers and her bill for the breast and back feathers. She quickly readjusted any feather that was out of place, running it through her bill and settling it neatly back in position.

'It will soon be time to leave,' said a voice from behind.

Sacer swivelled her head as Corvus and Granet glided over and perched beside her.

'Are you prepared?' asked Granet.

Sacer nodded and roused herself.

'Don't forget your worst enemy is the Nusham,' Granet continued, his voice hoarse with age. 'He has encroached on nearly all of our habitats. Death guns, traps and poisons are his weapons. Be vigilant!'

'Remember, by killing the racer you have earned their hatred,' added Corvus. 'There is now a price on your head. At least by leaving you will be defying the wrath of the hunters. You've learned well during the brief time we've spent together. You've got a taste of the harsh realities faced by our kind.'

Sacer nodded silently. The three of them watched the glow of sunrise and the exquisite freshness of the coming day. The sun was like a welcoming beacon.

'You'll always be welcome back to these Sacred Cliffs, my young friend,' said Granet. 'Your heart will tell you when it's time to return. Seek out Shimmer the rook. He'll introduce you to some dear friends in the lowlands – Kos the barn owl, Barkwood the long-eared owl, Crag the old fox, Bawson the badger, Vega the kestrel, Hotchiwichi the hedge-hog. All important friends and allies to the Council of Ravens.'

Then Sacer addressed the elders: 'I thank you, dear friends and teachers, for all your kindness and support. I will return, and I'll fulfill my birthright as a guardian of this sacred place.'

The elders stretched out their wings and spoke in unison:

'Father Sky, Mother Earth
Powers of the Universe
Protect Sacer
The noblest of Falcons
Enlighten, govern and guide her
Until she returns to us.'

The ravens nuzzled her neck and face with their strong bills. 'This is to reinforce our bonds of friendship,' Granet said. 'Farewell.'

Sacer rubbed against them gently, then moved over to the edge of the cliffs. Looking up at the cloudless blue sky, she opened her wings and gazed out over the great stretch of water. Facing the ravens again, she flexed her wings, then flapped away.

She felt honoured to have had such good teachers as the Council of Ravens. Then she began to think of the long journey ahead. She would be a stranger in a strange land. She felt strong enough to brave the perils of land and sea, but the Nusham – they were another story.

'The Nusham go down and down into darkness like a sinking ship in a bad storm.' Granet's words made her shudder as she pressed on, her feathers responding to the least pressure of the wind as she glided over the waves. 'You must move almost invisibly through life,' Corvus had told her. The gleaming radiant water dazzled her as she soared above the sea.

On through the soothing emptiness of the sky, across the vastness she journeyed in solitude, with no sound other than that of her wings and the waves.

Always alert, she enjoyed watching the manx shearwaters weave in and out above the waves as they passed by in flocks of twenty or more. Common terns hurried back to their young with beaks full of sand eels. The sheer delight of flight was so calming to Sacer that she quickly forgot her worries and just lived to fly. The day passed gently and quietly.

She remembered her father's words to her family as they had crouched so contentedly in their eyrie on the cliffs: 'Your wings were made for the wind.' Those words seemed so important now. When they were first said to her they had no meaning at all, but as she moved in the empty silence they became clear and true. She felt a twinge of sadness when she thought of her family. Some memories brought her sharp stinging pain. Yet there were also tender ones which made her happy.

Eyes fixed steadily, Sacer could see land ahead. Curlews were winging their way home across the crimson glow of sunset. Sacer circled, flapped across the swelling tide, past the waves that crashed against the rocks, then on towards a sandy beach where she alighted on a large boulder. She sat alert and watchful as darkness enveloped the landscape, listening to the melody of a song thrush rising and falling through the still evening. Exhausted, she slept soundly, lulled to sleep by the sound of the surf breaking gently on the shore.

* * *

Sacer awoke with a start as gulls wheeled and screamed overhead. Ring plovers ran along the water's edge, unaware of the falcon sitting like a sentinel on the tall rock. They were very active on the beach, preening, pausing, tilting forward to pick up crustaceans. As soon as Sacer roused herself, the ring plovers were away on quick wingbeat, calling in alarm, showing their broad white wing-bars and dark-tipped tails.

Herring gulls swooped at her several times, causing her to become increasingly anxious. She decided to take off and leave the place to the herring and black-headed gulls, who were scouring the bladder wrack and spiral wrack seaweeds for sand hoppers or kelp fly larvae.

As she sped away along wide stretches of beach a fresh breeze blew in from the sea and she felt a growing exhilaration. Her wings propelled her on in rhythmical, almost effortless beats, over the sand, across dunes, then higher, past spruce and fir trees. Startled starlings rose from the ground and quickly moved to safety as the falcon streamed overhead in the clear morning. They watched her black form against the sky as she moved away. They would not stir until they were sure she was truly gone.

Veering eastward, Sacer followed the course of a sparkling stream. Dragonflies hovered and darted about, intercepting smaller insects in mid-flight. Crouched among the rushes, a frog kept a watchful eye for predators and insects. A moorhen broke the calm of the water and hid among some rushes as the shadow of the falcon passed overhead.

Wheeling over fields that were splashed with the colours of wild flowers, Sacer flapped down and alighted on a fence-post where the stream joined the river. The air was sweet with the scent of flowers. Above, a skylark hovered and sang its lilting song, while his mate remained below, hidden among a galaxy of flowers.

Sacer suddenly caught sight of a Nusham at the far end of the river, but from her safe distance she did not feel too alarmed. The angler reeled in his line through the mirrored water. There were several splashes as he pulled on his rod, then he landed a fish and proudly displayed his catch to the air.

Tired from her long flight, Sacer sat and dozed in the warm sunlight. After some time, the loud noise of a train startled her as it thundered by on distant tracks. She took to the air again, soaring and circling, then spiralling on the up-drafts, winging her way high up over the river. The sun felt so good on her back. The winter months in the lowlands had been filled with fear and loneliness for her, but she felt so much more confident now.

Scanning below her, Sacer watched the swallows swoop gracefully to pick insects off the water. Wood-pigeons cooed from a horse chestnut tree. Sacer fluttered in the air as something caught her eye. She went into a long glide and descent. She was now flying tree-high above the river. What she had spied was a sleek-bodied otter moving sinuously downriver. It looked up at her inquisitively, whiskers and nostrils twitching, then in an instant it was gone. Sacer was away again high into the sky. The sky was her domain.

She began to think of the Council of Ravens and the words they had spoken from their *Sacred Book*:

> 'What mystery sets a heart beating
> Or a seed to grow into a flower?'

She would repeat that phrase over and over again in her mind. Sometimes it made her body tingle, as it created many images and feelings within her. But her favourite was the one her mother used to repeat:

> 'Love will always filter to the earth
> Like rays of sunshine or gentle rain.'

She knew that no matter how bad things might be, she could always hold on to these special thoughts.

Then the silence was broken by an assortment of sounds. She could see heavy dark smoke billowing out of chimney stacks, smudging the sky. Tall buildings loomed large against the skyline. The sun was now an orange ball as she flapped over an industrial sprawl. She hunched her wings and, dropping down, alighted on a gasometer. Nearby, the river looked dull as it cut its way through the city to meet the sea.

Sacer would sleep on an empty stomach, because now it was too late to hunt. Puffing up her feathers, she closed her big brown eyes.

CHAPTER 9

The Night Watch

As darkness came, Bawson the badger emerged from his sett. His kinfolk had all been out foraging since sunset, exploring the far side of the woods. As he slept alone in one of the chambers they rarely disturbed him, for they knew he would be a little grumpy and snappy if he was awakened too early. Still, he liked having them around and he always brought extra food for them, bits and pieces he would find along the verges of the road.

His stout plodding form moved through a quiet, silent glade. Stopping briefly, he looked out at the fields in the moonlight, remembering the most recent troubled dream he had, this time about his own clan. Maybe he was becoming a crank, always talking about doom and gloom. Well, he couldn't help his dreams. They just came to him uninvited.

He gave himself a good scratch, then he dug a latrine and, looking carefully about, did his dropping and scraped some earth over it. He cleaned himself meticulously and moved on along one of his well-trodden runways, halting near the edge of the woods to check for any danger.

Bawson sniffed the sweet-scented breeze that blew gently over the fields. He could hear the sound of horses breathing and snorting, then he could see others stamping their hooves and breaking into a gentle canter across the silvery fields.

He spied an owl moving as lightly as a shadow over the treetops.

'Night peace,' said a familiar voice.

Bawson looked around to see Barkwood swoop in and land on a post at the edge of the woods.

'How are you, dear friend?' asked the badger.

'Good!' said the owl warmly. 'I saw young Kos hunting over the barley fields earlier. The chicks have all hatched – a family of four.'

'That's good news,' said Bawson.

'How are all your clan?' enquired the owl.

'Big, strong and noisy,' chuckled the badger. 'Still, it's good to have them about the sett. It used to be so quiet and empty.'

The long-eared owl gave an alert glance behind him, ear tufts erect. He had detected movement.

'Night peace,' said old Crag. 'I can never manage to sneak up on either of you two.'

Barkwood ruffled his feathers and relaxed as the fox padded over to them.

'I seem to be becoming more noisy and less careful as I get older,' Crag continued. 'I'm like a young cub moving through the undergrowth.'

'I'm very distracted lately with all these dreams and visions,' sighed the badger. 'I've no good dreams any more, or if I do I can't remember them.'

'There was word from old Shimmer. I met him earlier, before sunset,' Crag interjected.

'How is he?' asked Bawson.

'Oh, fine,' replied Crag. 'He tells me there's a young

falcon due to arrive from the Sacred Cliffs any time now. He asked that we keep a lookout for her and extend her a warm welcome.'

'That sounds a bit worrying,' said the badger. 'Is there something wrong?'

'Don't alarm yourself, Bawson,' said the fox. 'It seems the Nusham are after her for killing one of their prize pigeons.'

'Nusham indeed!' grunted Bawson. 'It was the dark hour when they broke bonds with nature and forgot the ancient ways ...'

'Or ignored them,' remarked Crag.

Suddenly they heard frightened screams coming from a field nearby.

'What was that?' asked Bawson anxiously.

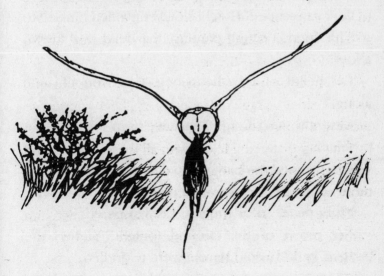

'It sounds like trouble,' said Crag.

They moved out slowly to investigate. There in the shadows was Hotchiwichi, all curled up, and twelve black rats trying to attack him.

The hedgehog stayed balled up as the persistent rats tried to uncoil him and expose his unprotected stomach. He sat in passive defence, his armoury of quills a strong shield against his enemies. The rats squealed and snapped, but to no avail. They were so determined in their efforts to make a meal of the hedgehog that they were totally unaware of the danger behind them.

With deadly speed, jaws and talons were brought into action, as owl, fox and badger rushed the rats, quickly distributing deadly bites and punctures. Two of the rats escaped. Hotchi slowly uncoiled himself to see his friends sitting panting, the dead rats strewn about.

'Oh, hello!' said the hedgehog. 'Glad you all came along.'

'City rats!' said Crag. 'I fear we're in for more rat problems.'

Kos, the barn owl, swooped down, holding a black rat in his beak, and dropped it alongside the others.

'Night peace, dear friends,' he whispered.

'Not much of that around tonight,' sighed the badger, as all his old terrors were rekindled.

CHAPTER 10

Changing Times

The birds in the falconry were restless. Moving fretfully on their perches, they watched each other closely. There were rumours, talk, but could it be true? The source was reliable. Sheila the heron always told the truth. She was a sure link with life outside the falconry. The cara cara had heard the same thing from the magpies, not that they could be trusted. Some of the birds in the falconry didn't even trust the cara cara, yet he was one of them, a prisoner, one of the longest-serving inmates of the place.

Wings flapped, heads bobbed. Some pulled at their jesses. Others, like the imperial eagle, pecked hard at themselves out of sheer frustration. The harsh scream of the tawny eagle made them more tense, and she called loudly for most of the morning. The fear and tension was felt in every joint and feather.

They were especially alert on this morning, staring over at the Nusham's house with fearful eyes. Owls, who would normally be asleep at this time, were peering out through the wooden laths. It was at times like this that they sorely missed the wisdom and calming words of Capella the golden eagle. But he was dead.

Things had never really been the same in the falconry since the passing of the golden eagle. Despite the fact that he was tied to his perch and had been a prisoner for so very long, Capella's words and stories could release their minds, keep the brightness in their eyes, and make them soar again when he spoke to them on warm summer evenings. They could imagine themselves flying free and wild, and despite the difficulties they faced he gave them all a sense of pride, a sense that they were noble birds from a distinguished race.

Now all that remained was fear and suspicion.

The bateleur eagle ruffled his feathers and raised his proud crest. What he had heard had sharpened his desire to be free. It had been planned for so long. He had become a close friend of the black vulture ever since the Nusham moved him to the block where the golden eagle once perched proudly.

The black vulture also wanted to escape, now more

than ever. If the falconry was closing down, as he had heard, he didn't fancy the idea of moving to some new place, whether it be a zoo or a falconry – having to adjust to a new life with strange birds for company. He felt too old for that kind of change, travelling in dark boxes; being handled by Nusham as they replaced jesses, trimmed his beak; being stared at and poked by young Nusham. No more, he thought. He was going home, back to Africa, or die in the attempt. Like the griffon vulture, he was prepared to take any risks. Come what may, he decided, he was going to be free.

The black vulture recalled what Capella had said to young Vega who had managed to escape from this dreadful place:

> 'When you leave here it's not only the
> fences that must disappear; the thoughts
> of being fenced must also be banished.'

Vega was young and had been capable of adapting to the wild again. But could he, a middle-aged vulture? And could he remove the fences from his mind if he did manage to escape? He gazed skyward and stretched out his mighty wings. Oh to be free, he sighed. To be unleashed. Instead of being earthbound he could be skyward. For in the sky he would find new dimensions of freedom. Only in the sky were the glories of a landscape revealed.

The falconry was a blend of slavery and freedom. While his body was tied to this perch his mind could soar the heights of freedom. Closing his eyes, the black vulture could imagine his dark wings climbing above the mountains. He could feel the ecstasy of the union of wings and wind hugging the sky. Inhaling deeply, he filled his lungs with the imaginary breath of freedom, as up and ever upwards he surged, clinging to the warm currents of an African sky.

The bark of the dogs brought his mind tumbling back to the falconry. Pulling himself alert, he ruffled his feathers as the Nusham walked up the gravel path with the three guard dogs. The man threw seven dead day-old chicks under his perch. The black vulture just sat there, motionless. The dogs barked loudly as the red-backed hawk flapped his wings and gave a sudden lunge forward.

'Quiet!' ordered the Nusham.

As eyes marked his passing, the birds grew increasingly anxious. Some of the smaller falcons and hawks cowered and shivered as they huddled on their perches. The tawny eagle started up his high-pitched scream when the Nusham came near. The dogs growled and snapped. The eagle crouched tense as he stared with accusing eyes.

What was compelling the birds to behave so? the falconer wondered. He had seen their various moods before, sensed their fears and frustrations. But now it was almost as if they knew that the place was closing. How could this be? he mused.

He had mixed emotions about selling up. He would miss the birds, but an offer of work in one of the finest falcon and hawk centres in the world could not be refused. He was looking forward to Italy, the facilities, the sunshine. It had so much going for it, while his own place was becoming very run down, had no money for expansion, and there was a falling-off in visitor numbers. Most of the birds were too old now, moth-eaten, as one of his friends said. Besides, it was difficult to get new birds. He had not been able to replace the golden eagle, the griffon vulture, the kites. Not that he was getting much for the sale of the remaining birds. It was really more a case of getting them off his hands.

Ten years was long enough in this place, the

falconer said to himself. He was making the right decision. These birds would be fine anywhere. They weren't pets. All they'd need would be food and a roof over their heads, and someone who could handle a hawk properly.

Hearing the phone ring he made a dash for the office, followed by the barking dogs.

The black vulture looked at the bateleur eagle. Nothing needed to be said. They knew they must escape, and soon.

CHAPTER 11

City Life

Sacer sat on a ledge watching the city awaken once again to the sound of traffic below. She could see the movement of thousands of Nusham streaming along the pavements. The roads were filled with cars, buses, and trucks rushing in noisy pursuit of each other. The sunlight glinted off the glass buildings. The concrete buildings and its ledges were like her cliffs.

Sacer felt hungry. Her dark brown eyes scanned the skyline for a meal. Flocks of starlings moved in small bands towards the park. Herring gulls screamed and hung low over the river. A cormorant, in deliberate strong flight, moved swiftly towards the sea. Sacer launched herself into the air. Higher and higher she rose, the warm breeze lifting her up into the clouds. She extended her wings so that she could glide slowly over the roof tops.

Below, there was a flurry of wingbeats as feral pigeons lifted off from the ground. Sacer fastened her eyes on them. Here was her chance. She felt her hunger keenly now as she had been without a meal for several days. Appraising the situation, her eyes locked on to the pigeon she would attack. She glided, wings still, waiting at the correct height. She focused her attention, head bobbing as she checked and planned every possible angle of attack. Her feathers quivered and her body tingled as her fierceness grew. The delectable pigeon circled around the plane trees.

Out from the sun the falcon came, into the attack at enormous speed, claws outstretched, talons hardened. This time she would succeed. With a dazzling swoop she stormed into the pigeon.

Sacer carried her prey back to the gasometer where she alighted and folded her wings. Gripping it tightly she plucked out the breast feathers until she reached the meat. Her sharp curved bill bolted down the meal. She ate in peace, the hunter's fire quenched. She had fed well. Satisfied now, she rested.

*   *   *

In the afternoon Sacer flew to the park and sat in a beech tree. When things became quiet and all the Nusham had left, she flew down to the pond and bathed at the edge. The ducks kept a safe distance. The water was cool and refreshing though she was careful not to get too wet. Then, ruffling her feathers, she shook her body and preened.

From an apple-blossom tree a female sparrowhawk watched for a time before flying down to join her. The peregrine pulled herself into an upright position.

'Are you new here?' enquired the sparrowhawk. 'I've observed you for several days hunting over the city. What makes one of your kind want to stay around here? Surely you'd prefer the mountains or the cliffs? Oh, I'm called Dawn, by the way. How about you?'

'Sacer,' the falcon replied, and went on to explain why she had to leave the Sacred Cliffs.

'The Sacred Cliffs? For most of the city birds all this would be legend. But you are living proof that such a place exists.

You *really* met the Council of Ravens? There are stories of a special Feather, with magic powers, which is supposed to be hidden there too.'

'I've seen it,' said Sacer proudly.

The sparrowhawk looked in awe at the falcon, threw a glance over her shoulder, then whispered in hushed tones 'You've actually seen it! It's real!?'

Sacer nodded. The sparrowhawk's eyes gleamed with excitement.

'Let's fly to the highest point of the city and there we can talk some more,' suggested Dawn.

They took to their wings and flapped away. A magpie called out in annoyance as they glided silently over the tallest building in the city. They perched in the calm still air, overlooking the river which divided the city. A blackbird's song floated up from the park.

'One can hear the sun rise and set in his voice,' whispered the sparrowhawk.

They watched a mute swan flying low over the water, the whistling sound of her majestic wings coming clearly to them as she sped away upriver.

'You've gladdened my heart,' said the hawk. 'For years I've held dear the stories of the Sacred Cliffs and all their mysteries. They're most important to me. Not many of the young birds today seem interested in tales and legends. All they want to do is eat, sleep and breed. Maybe city life does that.

Although I don't talk much about these things, I hold the thoughts in my mind.'

Sacer and the sparrowhawk felt a mutual admiration and respect which was impossible to explain since they were only briefly acquainted.

'"Some thoughts are greater than words." That's what my mother used to say,' remarked the falcon. 'It's from the *Sacred Book of Ravens*.'

'Really!' beamed the hawk. 'That's amazing. Tell me some more.' Her eyes widened as she made her request.

' "We must restore the world to peace and happiness ..." '

'That's a lovely notion, but an impossible task,' replied the hawk.

'Chapter eight Verse seven says:

> "Anger Pride and Hatred are enemies of
> love
> Without love there is no peace
> Without peace there is no happiness
> Without happiness there is only sorrow."

'Verse eight says:

> "All life forms can learn from each other
> The aim of knowledge is to produce
> Better understanding of each other."

'Verse nine says:

"Love, Compassion and friendship
Are the peaks we must soar to."

'Verse ten says:

"When the dark centres collapse
Because of their evil ways
Then the forces of light will flood
The planet. All will live in harmony." '

A look of deep thoughtfulness came over Dawn as she and Sacer remained in companionable silence, their perch burnished by the rays of the setting sun.

'Tomorrow I must find Shimmer the rook. Do you know him?' enquired Sacer.

'I've heard of him,' Dawn replied. 'You need to follow the river back inland. Look out for Sheila the heron. She works the river. She knows everything that's worth knowing.'

The light was fading fast as they bade each other farewell.

'It was so good to meet you, Sacer,' Dawn said. 'Perhaps we'll meet again.' Then lifting off, she flapped away across the dusky sky.

Sacer ruffled her feathers contentedly and flew off in the opposite direction, towards the gasometer. There she slept soundly for the night.

CHAPTER 12

Friend or Foe

Whizzer the crow moved with slow deliberate wingbeats across the morning sky. His task would be dangerous but he had the advantage of surprise on his side. King Spook had said he was the only one who could carry out this dangerous mission. That made him feel good. 'You're the ultimate winged assassin.' That's what the king had said. The mob had cheered in agreement.

With the Claw of Darkness in their grasp, the rats could return to their former greatness and he, Whizzer, would be up there alongside Hack, Spike and their leader.

'You shall reap the benefits,' King Spook had told him. 'When you destroy this falcon from the Sacred Cliffs you'll return to Ratland a conquering hero.

Be brave, bold and vicious. That's what is required and I know you won't let us down.'

Since the Nusham had not killed the falcon, Whizzer had suggested that *he* do the deed. King Spook agreed and applauded his deviousness. The last thing they wanted was a falcon turning up anywhere near Ratland, especially one connected with the Council of Ravens. It could only mean trouble. The falcon was probably full of revenge because the rats had killed two guardians of the Cliffs – she may even be their offspring, Hack had suggested.

King Spook may not have been endowed with as brutal a nature as Fericul and Natas, but he was skilled in deceit and cunning. Whizzer and the mob admired these traits. For King Spook, the Claw of Darkness had become his all-consuming passion, yet he had not used its powers. Soon he would.

Whizzer wanted to pave the way for him by getting rid of a potentially dangerous adversary. Whizzer knew that if the rats were to be the great conquerors of the earth he would be the only bird to share in their success. Fericul and Natas had craved power. King Spook had had it handed to him on a plate by a mysterious rat. The crow knew that Spook would use it wisely.

Suddenly the sky darkened and thunder attacked with heavy repeated claps. Clouds cracked as the thunder battered at the sky. Harsh rain swept behind the thunder, pelting down. Whizzer settled in a large oak tree to shelter from the storm.

* * *

Sacer sat in a Scot's pine and flicked her wings in a vain attempt to stop bluebottles wandering over them. The rain stopped as abruptly as it had begun. She sat relaxed, watching shafts of sunlight bore through the dark clouds. Rainwater dripped from the needles of the Scot's pine.

Sacer preened a little, then she lifted off from the

tree, her scythe-like wings taking her high into the sky. She turned on an uplift of air and scanned below her. The river was full now and moving at speed. Sacer was glad the city was behind her as she slanted away on the light breeze in search of Sheila the heron. She watched jackdaws jig and jerk in a distant field. Continuing to wheel and soar in the sky, eyes ever watchful, she noticed the hawk-like cuckoo flitting over some sedges. Sacer, savouring the silence, moved down hedge-high over barley fields that swayed and rippled in the breeze.

Sheila stood motionless among the sedges, watching Sacer approach. Pulling herself alert, she gave out a loud guttural cry. The peregrine alighted on a willow overhanging the river and looked across at the small lake where the heron stood.

'Are you Sheila?' asked Sacer.

'Who's enquiring?' demanded the heron.

'My name is Sacer. I've come from the Sacred Cliffs. I was told to find a rook named Shimmer.'

The heron lifted off and flapped her way over to the peregrine.

'So you're from the Sacred Cliffs? I suppose you know all the members of the Council of Ravens?'

'Well, some,' said Sacer 'My parents used to be guardians of the cliffs until they were killed by a renegade band of rats.'

The heron recoiled at the mention of rats, for she

had a vivid recollection of the confrontation between legions of them and herself and her friends.

'I remember those rats,' said Sheila. 'They were the fiercest and strongest we ever had the misfortune to encounter. We're all grateful that their reign of terror is over.' Then in a more haughty tone she asked why the peregrine should be looking for old Shimmer.

Sacer had to admit that she wasn't really sure. But she explained why she had to leave the cliffs, then added that Granet and Corvus suggested that she should look up their friends – Shimmer the rook, along with a fox, a hedgehog and a badger, some owls and a kestrel.

'No mention of me?' the heron asked, slightly annoyed.

'Well, no,' said Sacer. 'But a city sparrowhawk called Dawn told me of you.'

'Indeed!' remarked Sheila, who seemed very pleased that she should be known in the city.

Then the peregrine, sensing her pleasure, added: 'Yes. The sparrowhawk said, if anyone should know, it's Sheila the heron.'

'Well, I can't deny that,' replied the heron proudly. 'I'm privy to all the important news of the wildfolk. Now, follow the river for another couple of bridges, then look out for the big house, where some Nusham live. Don't worry. They rarely bother us. Nearby you will discover Shimmer's rookery. It's easy to find because it's always teeming with noisy rooks. The young ones are the loudest of course. Well, no doubt we'll meet again, if you're planning to stay around these parts. Do take care. I know you'll soon meet up with all the friends the ravens have spoken about. Farewell!'

Sacer was airborne again, glad of the encounter with the heron. She knew that if Corvus and Granet had recommended Shimmer and his friends then she had nothing to worry about except the Nusham. She had adjusted quickly to life alone, but was always grateful for company when she found it.

Now, bizarre thoughts rose unbidden to the surface of her mind. She felt tension, a sense of foreboding. But why? The same distress was seizing her now as when she was told that the Nusham were after her. Yet all seemed well. Why should she be so troubled?

She skirted over a small wood, across more fields, over farm buildings and tall trees, scanning below, watching. Cattle grazed in the fields; rabbits emerged from their burrows to nibble in the buttercup meadows. Calm and peaceful. But Sacer continued to be troubled.

A harsh *kaaah, kaaah, kaaah* rasping call startled the peregrine. She looked over her shoulder, and her flight suddenly faltered, as out from a copse of spruce and fir trees a hooded crow came. Sacer circled apprehensively.

'Greetings!' cawed Whizzer. 'Welcome to the low-lands.'

Sacer was puzzled, but pleased at encountering another friendly bird. They flew alongside each other high over the river.

'You have come from the Sacred Cliffs and are seeking old Shimmer. Correct?' asked the crow.

Sacer nodded, wondering how the hooded crow knew where she had come from and what her intention was.

'Do you know the Council of Ravens?' she asked, as she beat a little more slowly to stay alongside the crow.

'Yes. I have met them all. Corvus, Granet and the elders.'

Sacer relaxed at this and she enquired how he knew she was looking for Shimmer and the friends. 'Did Sheila the heron tell you?' she asked.

'Yes,' replied Whizzer. 'She told me to escort you to the rookery. Not that such a powerful falcon as yourself would be in much danger of being attacked. But sometimes if the rooks see a strange bird, especially a hawk or falcon, they'll harry it without mercy. However, there's no need to worry, now that I'm with you, because I'm known to all the important rookeries in the area.'

With that the hooded crow appeared to waver in flight.

'What is it?' asked Sacer, sensing the crow was bothered.

'Up ahead. On the wires. Seven magpies.'

Sacer had already seen them, but was not perturbed. She had been mobbed several times before by those annoying birds as she hunted along the estuaries during the winter months.

'We'd better head for the old quarry. Quick. Follow me,' ordered the crow.

Sacer did not argue but sped away towards the quarry. There they alighted near the edge, on a large boulder and looked around to check that they weren't being followed.

'It'll be safe here for the time being,' said Whizzer. 'Those magpies work for the Nusham. He has a falconry where he traps noble birds – hawks, eagles, kites, harriers, buzzards and owls. He even has some of your kind. Prisoners. Every one of them. They'll never escape from there. If the magpies see you they'll surely report it. Next thing traps will be set and as sure as eggs are eggs the Nusham'll catch you. Then you'll end up as one of his prize exhibits – which is why I take such precautions to protect you until you're safely among your friends.'

'You're a good friend,' said Sacer. 'Someday I'll tell the Council of Ravens about your kindness.'

'We should rest here and tomorrow before sunrise I'll lead you to Shimmer,' concluded the crow.

Sacer ruffled her feathers and gazed across at the darkening landscape. Sitting on the ledge reminded her of the cliffs where she had been born. It was comforting. She watched a skein of duck taking their last flight of the evening across the pink-tinged sky before settling in a nearby lake.

'Rest now,' urged Whizzer. 'You must be tired after your long flight from the city. I'll keep watch until starlight, then I too will rest.'

Sacer roused herself, stretched luxuriously, a wing at a time, then settled down for a good sleep.

* * *

As night rolled in Whizzer planned his deadly deed. Picking up a heavy, sharp stone with his beak he turned to the dozing Sacer and with all the strength he could muster crashed the stone on to the falcon's back. Sacer felt an excruciating pain from the blow, then ... only darkness.

Whizzer watched the peregrine somersault, then tumble, as she plummeted to the bottom of the quarry. The crow looked over the ledge, watched, waited, listened. Silence from below. Whizzer cawed with diabolical glee. Mission accomplished! A direct assault and it was all so easy!

Eyes flashing wildly, Whizzer launched himself into the air, Ratland bound.

CHAPTER 13

Harbinger of Death

A cacophony of high-pitched yelps and squeals could be heard as King Spook entered the centre chamber. Hordes of rats were glutting themselves on food brought back by the different raiding parties. Bread, sausages, a variety of fruits, chickens, beef, eggs, a teal, a pheasant, two moorhens, a male mallard and a piglet, plus lots of songbirds. Hack and Spike looked greatly pleased with the orgy of eating and the variety and abundance of food; they were the quartermasters whose duty it was to organise the provisions.

The piglet was prepared for King Spook, Hack and Spike. Gobbling lips and sharp yellow teeth nibbled greedily and furtively, tearing mouthfuls of meat from the tender piglet. Regurgitating food spilled from the side of Spook's mouth as he complimented Hack and Spike on the delicious fare.

The chambers echoed with merriment as rats, mice and shrews swarmed in and out, squirming, chewing and gnawing their way through the banquet. Hunched on their hindquarters, doe rats sang merry songs while the bucks performed rodent dances.

Hack had clamped his jaws around a teal's leg and begun to feed when he noticed Whizzer entering. 'Your Majesty,' he reported to Spook. 'Whizzer is here.'

King Spook lifted out his head from the side of the piglet and greeted the crow. With snouts twitching and fur stiffened, the mob waited on risen haunches to hear what Whizzer had to relate.

'The deadly deed is done,' he announced. 'The falcon is no more.'

Spook's eyes widened and he danced a frenzied dance around his throne. Wriggling and leaping over each other the rodent mob joined him, the floor suddenly alive with moving shapes. They yelped, screamed and squealed in celebration of victory.

When they had all settled down again and eaten their fill Spook rested on his throne and spoke: 'My dear subjects, you'll agree we've now attained a good quality of life down here in our ancient home of Ratland.' There were loud cheers. 'Since you think I'm worthy to be your king I'd like to share something with you.

'We've been given a special gift which will shield us from our enemies. Indeed, not only will it shield us but it may destroy them.'

More loud cheers echoed through the chambers.

'Good Spike, bring in our secret weapon.'

The rodents wondered what secrets might be revealed. Twitching and grimacing, they knocked and nudged for position.

In trembling awe Spike carried in the Claw of Darkness. A tide of fear rose in the mob as they stared at its grotesque shape. The strange green fog pouring from the bizarre object only compounded their fears. They burst into fits of shaking and began to hug one another for security.

With a sarcastic gleam in his eyes, Spook told them not to be afraid. The nightmarish light circled the chamber. Spook broke into mocking laughter: 'This, my subjects, will not harm us.'

Holding the Claw aloft for a moment, then carefully replacing it on the carved stone, he continued: 'But it will harm our enemies. Let me explain.' They gathered around the throne and stared hard at the Claw. With boastful confidence King Spook stretched out his arms. The green light swirled and circled in rhythm with Spook's arm movements.

'We must never waver in our decision,' he shrieked, as if possessed. 'We must ensnare our enemies ... then destroy them.' He grimaced. There was a rush of ghostly air which made them all shudder.

King Spook seemed oblivious. His eyes widened with sheer delight. 'See!' he squealed. 'Look there!' His expression was now calmer, but sinister nonetheless. 'Look what I've conjured up. This is the pool of enchantment.'

They stared into the pulsating, bilious green light, wide-eyed and fear-stricken. 'It's time to show the power of the Claw.'

Silent and awe-struck they sat, not knowing what to expect.

Whizzer, Hack and Spike glanced at one another. Spook seemed more like Fericul or Natas than his old self.

'All we have to do now is think of our enemies.'

'A barn owl!' shouted Hack nervously.

Spook's eyes flashed. 'A barn owl? Good! Our first victim will be a barn owl.' The hideous green fog revealed a barn owl flying over a field.

The rodents watched and waited to see what would happen.

* * *

Across the twilight sky flew Driad, searching the fields for a meal. With soundless flight he passed over the meadow. He could hear the murmur of the river but no rustle of mouse or rat. To his right the lake shimmered in the moonlight. He moved like a shadow across the field, hovering for a time, then moving on. Still no sign of any rodents. Earlier he had tried to catch a bat, but without any luck.

Snowdrop was becoming broody again, especially since she heard Crannóg had hatched eggs.

In their first season together they had raised a family of four. That was more than four seasons ago. Well, if there was a chance of another family he must build up a larder. It was their way of bonding the relationship, proving that he was a good provider while she would sit brooding their eggs.

Driad thought about his younger brother Kos having his very own family. So much had happened to the two brothers since their young days in Donadea Castle. Now that draughty old castle was alive again with the sound of owlets hissing and snoring.

Driad slipped into a glide over the moonlit fields. Up ahead he could see old Bawson the badger, edging out from the shadows of the woods. He hunched his wings and dropped down on to a post. The badger was startled by the sudden appearance of the owl.

'Night peace, Kos,' whispered Bawson.

'Night peace to you, Bawson. Only I'm Driad, not Kos.'

'Oh yes,' smiled the badger. 'Silly me. But you two look rather alike, don't you think?'

'Well, it's only to be expected, being brothers and all that!' Driad then explained that he had been on the wing since dusk and had not seen one mouse or rat while searching the fields and along the river.

'They're around somewhere, that's for sure,' growled the badger. 'They attacked Hotchi the hedgehog last evening and it was only sheer luck that Crag, Kos, Barkwood and myself came along. It was those city rats too, up to no good, you can be sure. Well, we finished them off but there are hordes more. I know. They could be watching us right now.' Bawson trembled at the thought of it. 'Do you dream?' he asked, his body now rigid.

'No!' said Driad.

'Well, I do. And lately my dreams have all been bad. The moon turning red with blood ... then the Grey Owl floating by ...'

Driad began to feel edgy. 'Listen, Bawson, I must away. I want to build up a store of food. We are thinking of having a second brood.'

Bawson recoiled as if he had seen something terrible. His eyes widened and he started twitching uncontrollably.

'Are you all right?' asked Driad.

'I have seen terrors that will shake the heart,' Bawson blurted out.

'I think you should go back to your sett and rest,' said Driad. 'You may be coming down with a fever.'

'Do you think so?' asked Bawson hopefully. 'Perhaps you're right. I haven't been sleeping too well lately. Maybe a drink from the cool stream, then a good sleep ... that might do the trick ...'

The badger moved away slowly, his mind apparently tortured with troubled thoughts. He suddenly turned back to the owl: 'Don't hunt tonight, Driad. Please! Just go home to Snowdrop. Hunt tomorrow night.' His eyes were glazed. He turned and trundled off, past the dark foliage of the hedgerow, towards the woods.

The owl slipped away to probe the night once more. Quartering the fields, he considered Bawson's words. They made him tense. He shivered, then shook his body in a bobbing motion and tried to put the thoughts out of his mind. Skirting hedgerows, he looked to the silver moon, noting gladly that there was no red to be seen. The sky was ignited with stars, just the perfect night for foraging. He gave a loud shriek. Perhaps it would startle some rodents from their hiding places and make them scurry somewhere else. It usually worked. Skimming over thick gorse that bordered the motorway, he alighted on a tree stump. Then he watched and waited in the soft night light.

Driad was sorry he had met old Bawson because he was now full of fear and discomfort. The badger had foretold things before and he had the uncanny gift of foreseeing disasters and tragedies. Yet Driad was hungry and was only obeying the call of instinct. He began to think more pleasant thoughts, of the happy day when he first met Snowdrop ... it was the season when the bracken unfolds its tight green fronds ...

Suddenly he was assailed with more troubled thoughts. He recalled how Snowdrop too had asked him not to venture out tonight. She had wanted him to sit alongside her in the moonlight and just watch the sky. He had teased her, saying she should have picked Kos as her mate, for that was more his style of things. Still, he'd promised he wouldn't stay out too late, because there had been a lot of Nusham activity near their roost. Snowdrop thought another Nusham track was being planned.

Driad decided to try along the verge of the motorway. That was always a sure place to catch little furries, and afterwards he would head back home. With silent flight he began to patrol the rough verges. Gently he flapped along. In an instant a brown rat emerged from some long grass. Driad hovered, then dropped like a stone. The rat gave a high-pitched squeal. Driad transferred the rat to his bill, carried it to a post and fed.

Lights bore through the velvet darkness as cars, lorries and trucks hurtled past. Eyes ever watchful, Driad scanned the ground. If he could catch two more rats he'd manage to carry them home. He crouched, tense, checking around. A movement caught his eye. He turned swiftly. Up ahead, sniffing through a mound of debris, were five rats. It would be dangerous to attack so many, so he must plan carefully.

Speed and cool-headedness were required here. His wings found the air. He needed height. The rats were busy feeding on a dead cat, unaware that the owl hovered above them, ready to strike. Suddenly a juggernaut thundered past. The slipstream pulled Driad out over the motorway. His body wavered, swaying and weaving. He tried to adjust his position. Lights bore through the darkness, white, yellow, amber. Driad was completely dazzled. Jerking his body, he tried to flap to the safety of the verge, but

his eyes locked on to gleaming lights that moved at frightening speed. He made an abortive attempt to fly.

There was a thud.

'Bloody hell!' yelled the driver. 'What was that? Nearly smashed my windscreen!' He glanced back, but could see nothing.

Driad's twisted form kicked and struggled for life.

As the grey light that preceded dawn streaked the sky the lifeless body of a barn owl could be seen on the grassy verge.

CHAPTER 14

Reign of Terror

*S*acer wiped her bill on the log. Her hunger satisfied, she preened and stretched luxuriously. The stinging pain had gone from her head and she felt refreshed and invigorated. Now in the dimming light she could see something moving and she began to have twinges of apprehension.

The hedgehog plodded over to her and sniffed around her feet. 'All's well again,' remarked Hotchi. 'I see you have your appetite back. That's very good. Of course, Crag, Barkwood and Bawson supplied the meals. And it was young Kos and myself who found you. Thought you were dead. You certainly looked it.'

The falcon tried to remember what had happened. 'I was with a hooded crow. He brought me to the quarry for safety. Said he knew Shimmer. Offered to show me his rookery. Then I felt a thump. Next thing I remember is waking up here. There was food strewn about, so I ate it.'

'There's only one hooded crow who'd behave like that and it's Whizzer. A rogue, that one!' muttered the hedgehog.

Just then Crag arrived on the scene, sniffed the air and padded over to Sacer. 'Glad to see you up again. Sheila the heron told us all about you.'

Barkwood and Kos arrived together. 'Night peace, everyone.' They glided down and perched alongside Sacer.

'How did I get here?' asked Sacer.

'Thanks to Hotchi and Kos. They found you in the quarry,' said the fox.

Kos filled in all the blanks for her. 'It was Crag who brought you safely here, and sat keeping vigil. You've been out of it for over two nights. Asleep, I mean! You were very fortunate to fall on the brambles and not on the sharp rocks. Shimmer has been here twice to see you, and he's asked the rooks to keep a lookout for that hooded crow.'

'Well, all I can say is thank you all for your kindness,' said Sacer. 'Someday I hope to be able to repay it. Of course, you all come highly recommended by the Council of Ravens.' The friends looked pleased.

Suddenly Bawson came crashing out from the undergrowth, startling everyone.

'What's the matter, dear friend?' asked Crag.

All eyes fixed on the badger as tears spilled down his cheeks.

'It's the darkest of nights,' Bawson sobbed.

Crag nudged him tenderly.

Bawson moved away on his own and turning slowly he looked first at Kos. 'It's my disagreeable duty to tell you that your brother Driad was killed last evening on the motorway.'

There was a stunned silence. He slunk away a little further. 'Crag, dear friend,' he sobbed the words, 'two of your own, young Asrai and Redwind, were found earlier by Longears the hare. Strangled by those accursed hedgetraps.'

The terrible pain of grief bore down on them. Crag gave a pitiful yelp. The little group sat silently under the clear sky, wracked with misery.

'We fall like leaves in the wind,' sighed Crag. He sat in the deep grass under a lime tree. He thought of his young, now dead. He thought also of his dead mate, Asrai, recalling her lovely form emerging from the shady entrance to the den. Closing his eyes, he could almost smell her sweet scent along the fern path.

Almost immediately his nose twitched as a new smell filtered into it. It couldn't have been worse. It was the smell of death, creeping through the woods. Grim thoughts burdened the friends as Bawson yelled

loudly: 'It's the choking death. It's in the woods.'
Morbid images came streaming out relentlessly.

'We haven't a moment to lose,' urged Crag as he
headed towards the ghastly smell. They froze in their
tracks as they came through the clearing near
Bawson's sett. They found the sett surrounded by
three Nusham.

The friends lurked in the shadows, observing the
Nusham warily.

'I thought the badgers around here were all
healthy,' remarked one of the Nusham. 'Can't take any
chances though. I don't want my cattle infected
because of some wild badgers.'

They waited until the Nusham left before moving
out towards the sett. The death smell was everywhere, stinging their eyes, choking their breathing.
Bawson trembled. He knew only too well what that
gas meant.

As dawn broke over the trees
Crag and Hotchi went
down into the sett.

There was only one entrance open. The chambers were silent as the grave. The odour of death filled their nostrils. They were appalled by the sight that met their eyes.

Huddled together in one chamber were the lifeless forms of five badgers. Bawson sat there beside them, sobbing uncontrollably.

'What a sad end to the Straffan Clan,' sighed Hotchi.

CHAPTER 15

The Closing of the Falconry

The birds watched the removal van arriving at the gate.

'Nice morning,' said the driver.

'Aye. We've been lucky with the weather these past few weeks,' remarked the falconer.

'I hear you're heading off to Italy.'

'Yes. Next Saturday.'

'I'd love to see Rome,' said the driver.

'Um. I'll be near Florence. I'm going to be working with birds there.'

'You must have a way with them,' laughed the driver.

'Come in for a coffee before we get started,' said the falconer.

As he opened the office three dogs came out

barking. The driver stepped nervously away. 'Quiet!' shouted the falconer. 'They won't touch you,' he said to the driver.

The driver stared hard at the two rottweilers and the black labrador. 'Sure glad I'm not your postman.' They laughed and went inside.

The black vulture watched the office door close. He'd dreaded this day, while at the same time yearning for it. It was now or never, he thought, staring at the other birds who had resigned themselves to the inevitable. The black vulture had bitten through the leather thongs which bound him to the perch.

'Are you ready?' he asked the bateleur eagle, who'd been working steadily on the long cord imprisoning him.

'Ready!' said the eagle. He shivered with anticipation, thinking of the warm sun of their homeland, looking forward to gliding over the savannahs. 'Yes, it's the pleasant thoughts of home that keep me going,' he whispered.

The cara cara moved nervously on his perch, eyes ablaze with fear. The red marker beside his name worried him greatly. Markers had been carefully placed on some birds' names and not on others. Why was that? he wondered. Even the magpies didn't know what the markers meant. They lived at the edge of the falconry and gave him all the news, whether or not he gave them food in return.

The driver came out of the office and began to take wooden boxes from the back of his van.

'I'll be with you in a moment. I must change the jesses on this peregrine,' said the falconer.

'Take your time,' the driver called back. 'I'm in no hurry.' He walked around looking at the different birds. They gazed uneasily back at him. When he came to the cara cara he thought, what a pity to put down such fine specimens. Eight out of forty birds had the red marker. Well, I'm sure the vet knows what he's talking about, he said to himself. The rest of the birds would go to zoos, wildlife parks and private collectors.

* * *

Spook looked at the birds through the green pool. He sniggered wildly.

'See, my loyal subjects. More enemies. We have destroyed one owl, two foxes and five badgers. Now let's have some fun with these big birds. They want to be free from bondage. Well, we can arrange that.' There was a new ferocity in his eyes. Gone was the old nervous Spook the other rats liked.

'I think we will use the dogs to make a violent, swift, savage attack.' He sniggered loudly. 'Our campaign of collective terror is paying dividends.' His eyes alighted on the mysterious Claw. 'Do your worst!' He was seething with evil passion.

* * *

Within the falconry, the dogs suddenly became still, as if spellbound, and their eyes began to glow red. Terror gripped the watching birds. The driver stopped in his tracks. The dogs growled, fang-toothed, drooling green spittle. Then, making low menacing noises, they moved closer and closer. Suddenly they tore into the air, eyes flashing wildly, jaws snapping. Shrieks and screams of birds being torn apart by savage teeth rent the air.

The falconer emerged from his office to find his dogs had become hideous monsters running amok. Attempting to assess the situation and get it under control, he rushed inside, got his shotgun and immediately emptied both barrels into the dogs. Quickly reloading, he fired a further two rounds. The dogs were flung across the lawn with the force of the blasts. Their bodies jerked and flinched and then were still.

The driver stood trembling, aghast at what he had just witnessed. The falconer quickly checked the birds that had been attacked. Twelve dead.

'I've never witnessed anything like it,' he said.

The driver, still shaking, followed him to his office. From there the falconer called the vet.

'What a thing to happen!' said the bateleur eagle. 'What are we going to do?' he pleaded with the black vulture.

'There's nothing we can do here. Let's get away. Are you coming?'

The eagle looked around at the carnage: the imperial eagle lying dead alongside the goshawk; the red-backed hawk, the kite, and the cara cara torn to pieces, along with the red-tailed hawk, two sparrowhawks, a kestrel, the common buzzard, an eagle owl and a merlin. All savaged to death.

'Come on!' yelled the black vulture.

With a rush of wings they exploded from their perches, flapping wildly, chopping the air to gain height. They flew skywards, away over the falconry. No one even noticed their escape except the barred owls, who wished them a safe journey.

The next day the local papers' headlines read: 'Rabid Dogs Savage Prize Hawks'.

The vet performed autopsies on the dogs but found no trace of rabies or any other unusual disease.

When the other birds were taken away in the wooden crates the falconer and the vet built a fire and burned the carcasses of the dogs and the dead birds.

* * *

Hack looked at King Spook and noticed his eyes. He whispered to Spike to look.

'What is it?' demanded Spook, becoming aware that they were staring at him.

'Well, your Highness, it's your eyes.'

'What about them?' he snarled.

They held a piece of broken mirror up to his face. Spook took hold of it and saw fierce red eyes stare back at him from the mirror. He screamed in horror, dropping the mirror which shattered into pieces. 'What's happening to me, comrades? What am I becoming?'

'It's not you, King Spook, but that!' said Hack, pointing to the Claw of Darkness.

Its mocking presence and heavy green fog seemed to ooze evil and to engulf all who came in contact with it and its dark ways.

CHAPTER 16

Hibou, the Wise One

A sad silence hung over the woods. The news about Driad, the Straffan badgers, Crag's offspring and the birds from the falconry was almost too much to bear. The shock of that final loss which death brings bore down heavily on the wildfolk, and it was several days before they were out and about again.

After a decent interval Crag called a meeting. He had yelped a message to his friends on the previous night. Barkwood was the first to arrive. Then Bawson appeared. He had been sleeping under the rhododendrons since the death of his clan. Hotchi came immediately after. Hares, rabbits, stoats, otters, squirrels, and birds arrived from all their various forms, warrens, holes, holts, dreys and nests. Even sworn enemies put their differences to one side in order to be at this important meeting.

Sacer had slept nearby, but was now perched silently alongside Shimmer. Kos had gone to comfort Snowdrop; he would try to persuade her to come and live with Crannóg and himself in the castle. Vega had flown several miles to be at the meeting. He arrived with Sheila the heron. The fox padded around in a small circle, nodding greetings to everyone. Sparrowhawks, woodcocks, woodpigeons, stock doves, pheasants, jackdaws, jays, magpies and songsters – all sat about the trees, silently staring.

'Let's call the meeting to order,' said the hedgehog. 'Crag will now address the assembly.'

The fox broke into a sad smile. 'Thank you, Hotchi. It's a sad time for us all. I know most of you have been touched by grief in some form or other. Life seemed so much happier in those long green seasons of our youth. To pad the woodland path, the scents of spring filling our nostrils; the delicious thrill of surprise when we discovered something new; the moonshine that would light up an avenue of trees.'

The creatures watched the fixed shine in Crag's eyes. He seemed self-absorbed. His voice was commanding and reassuring; he had a way of creating a soothing stillness. There he sat, hunched in the silvery light.

'It now seems that we've been plunged into total

darkness. Our minds and hearts are burdened with death images.' His sorrowing amber eyes appeared pierced through with pain. Then he looked to the sky and spoke gently: 'How lucky is a star hanging serenely in the heavens, bright and untroubled.' He tried to hold back the tears. There was an empty silence as sadness shadowed them all.

Then Sacer spoke:

> 'Without the gifts of love and friendship
> We would drown in confusion and darkness ...'

These words touched them deeply. Everyone turned to Sacer. 'It's from the *Sacred Book of Ravens*,' she whispered.

'You've turned the tides of sadness,' said Crag.

'And without friends,' added the hedgehog, 'you'd end up talking to yourself.'

This comment brought hoots of laughter from Bawson. The others relaxed and laughter flooded through their beings, bubbling up into tears of relief, which flowed until they all felt a final happy exhaustion.

After things had settled down and the deadly tension of grief was finally broken, Barkwood spoke: 'I think there's something very sinister behind these tragedies, all coming so close upon each other.'

'What do you mean?' asked Vega.

'I think there's a war being waged against us, and

I suspect the rats are involved,' said Barkwood. 'They've tried to bring chaos and anarchy before and I fear they'll succeed if we don't get help to defend ourselves from these constantly threatening menaces. I'm convinced the driving force behind this evil is the rats ...'

They all sensed Barkwood's words were true.

'What do you suggest, dear friend?' asked Crag.

'I think we should visit Hibou, the wise one of the ancient forest,' offered Barkwood.

Among the friends only Crag and Bawson had ever heard of Hibou.

Barkwood explained that Hibou was an eagle owl, the last of his kind, who lived in the ancient oak forest. 'His ancestors have been there since the forest was young. He's the one with all the wisdom and wood-lore. He has at times advised the Council of Ravens when there were important decisions to be made. But now he tends to keep to himself and is rarely seen. It was my parents who told me of his existence, and how the Nusham tried to hunt him down with death guns and traps, but they never succeeded.'

'You're sure he's still there?' enquired the hare.

Barkwood admitted that he had never seen him, and had no idea whether he was alive or dead, but felt it was worth finding out.

Crag agreed and said they could not let things go on as they were.

Sacer, Barkwood, Shimmer, Hotchi, Crag, Vega and Bawson decided to make the journey. While they were gone, all the other wildfolk would be extra vigilant in case of any attacks. Sheila said she would inform Kos if she saw him.

'We'd better snatch a few hours' rest,' suggested Hotchi. 'It's preferable to travel refreshed and invigorated, don't you agree?'

'You're a wealth of wisdom,' smiled Crag.

The seven who were to travel said farewell to their friends and went off to rest.

* * *

'It's time, dear friend, to go,' said the fox.

Bawson yawned and stretched. It was the first good rest he'd had in ages.

Barkwood nudged the hedgehog.

'Oh, is it morning already?' asked Hotchi, plucking a leaf off his spines.

Sacer looked at the rose-pink streaks across the morning sky then preened her breast feathers. Shimmer stretched his wings and flapped. Vega sat high in a pine tree keeping a lookout.

Crag, Bawson and Hotchi moved quietly through the undergrowth, while the four birds flew out and waited at the edge of the woods. The rookery was awakening. Shimmer looked at the young ones circling the trees. He couldn't tell them where he was going or when he would be back. They were flying well and, as usual, were very noisy. Below, cattle grazed in the fields.

For a time the birds moved in silence over the rolling meadows and across sloping fields. Sometimes they would circle and wheel in the sky, so as not to travel too far from their friends who had to make the journey on foot. This is a good way to become acquainted with Shimmer, Barkwood and Vega, Sacer said to herself. Shimmer had the wisdom of age on his side and knew when to fly and when to sit in a tree and wait.

The sun shone brightly out of a clear blue sky. A yellowhammer sang from the top of a telegraph pole. Speckled wood butterflies danced over the hedges. Bumblebees were visiting the tall purple foxglove that grew on the bank.

The hedgehog sniffed among the herb robert and the yellow lady's bedstraw and came out crunching a ground beetle. A hoverfly began to annoy him.

'Shoo!' snapped Hotchi.

Crag rested for a while and licked his fur, removing some thistle and ragged robin.

Bawson disturbed a flock of sheep, and they raced down the fields. Oh dear, I didn't mean to worry them, he thought to himself. That's the kind of thing the Nusham would notice. Bawson continued to grub for worms for a time. Onwards they moved through thicket and ferns.

Crag watched rabbits emerge from their warren to crop the short sweet grasses, but he had no desire to hunt. He had lost his appetite. He could see Vega hovering up ahead, eyes scanning the ground for the slightest movement. Eventually there was an explosion of action as the kestrel caught a long-tailed fieldmouse.

'These youngsters have an inexhaustible wellspring of energy, don't you agree, Bawson?' remarked Crag.

'Oh, for the carefree days of youth!' smiled the badger.

They had travelled a great distance that day; it was now time to rest. Crag, Bawson and Hotchi were paw weary. The birds flew back to join them. Still no sign of the ancient forest. They sat overlooking grassy meadows and watched the soft light of evening creep in. Sacer preened her deep cream breast and wings, then extended her bright yellow legs. The fox trotted down to a nearby stream and soothed his paws in the cool water. The badger joined him.

'That feels so good,' said Crag as he immersed himself, lapping up some water. 'I'm afraid we are getting older and slower.'

'Too true,' sighed Bawson.

Across the velvet dusk Barkwood saw Kos flapping silently over swaying barley fields. The long-eared owl gave several hoots. Kos sped over and landed in an ash tree.

'Night peace,' whispered the barn owl.

'It gladdens our heart to see you again,' said Crag.

'I brought Snowdrop back to live in the castle,' said Kos. 'She seems to be bearing up well.'

'How's the family?' asked Barkwood.

'All fine. The owlets are getting bigger and stronger. Crannóg and Snowdrop are working the fields together. There's enough food for two broods, they're both such excellent providers. So here I am. Crannóg insisted I come.'

'We're all glad you're here,' said Crag.

A light rain began to fall. Crag, Bawson and Hotchi settled down under a hedge, listening to the pattering rain dripping from the leaves. The birds sheltered together in a nearby ash tree.

Next morning as they passed alongside a young conifer plantation a large brown owl-like bird rose from the ground and soared into the air. She gave out a loud harsh *kek-kek-kek* call as she circled them. It was a hen harrier.

'We come in peace,' announced Barkwood.

The hen harrier circled a second time, staring hard at Sacer, who could be the most threatening to her family. Then the fox called: 'We've come to see the great wise owl Hibou. Can you help us?'

Sacer dropped from the sky and alighted on a fence-post, to show she had no intention of doing battle. Vega followed suit. Barkwood hovered with

Kos and they too dropped down on to the fence. The hen harrier wavered, then she dropped down into the field.

Crag stretched out in a relaxed pose. Bawson sat behind him.

Hotchi trundled up to the harrier: 'This is Shimmer, the leader of one of the oldest rookeries in the land.' Shimmer nodded to the harrier. 'Sacer over there,' continued the hedgehog, 'was born on the Sacred Cliffs and knows the Council of Ravens personally. So do I, for that matter. Barkwood is—'

'We're on a mission,' Crag interrupted, 'a very important one, and we must speak with Hibou, the wise one.'

'I was about to say all that,' grumbled Hotchi.

'You're near the great forest. You should be there by evening,' said the hen harrier.

'How will we find Hibou,' asked Shimmer, 'in such a vast forest?'

'If he decides to meet with you he'll locate you,' was the hen harrier's reply.

'You mean, he may not wish to talk?' asked a worried Hotchi.

'He is lord of the forest. He'll decide,' said the hen harrier. 'Now I must leave, for we've been having serious trouble in these parts. My mate was killed on the night of the waning moon.'

'What happened?' asked Bawson.

'We were attacked by a raiding party of rats.'

'Rats!' exclaimed the friends.

'Yes,' said the hen harrier. 'City rats and brown rats. Hordes of them invaded the area several times. Most of the songsters were attacked. Eggs and young were taken. They didn't stop there either. Pheasants, partridge, hawks, pigeons and ducks all suffered heavy losses. There were even raids on farms. This angered the Nusham and they have laid poison. As a result foxes, badgers, owls and even cats and dogs have been poisoned indirectly.'

Bawson shivered at the prospect of future battles.

The hen harrier explained that the past few days had been trouble-free but she remained cautious. She offered them some food from her secret larder, for which they were very grateful.

Thanking her, they went on their way.

Leaving familiar territory brought pangs of apprehension as the strange urgency they all felt pressed them silently onwards. Moving in the warm sun through long swaying grasses, a waft of sweet honeysuckle, carried on the gentle breeze, filled their nostrils.

There was a gloomy stillness as they approached the great forest. Their eyes met in growing wonder at the majesty and beauty of the place. The forest was blanketed by an evening mist. Shafts of golden sunlight slanted through the trees. There was a sense of increasing awe as they went along the forest path. The trees rose around them like mighty pillars. They looked up along the imposing trunks and sensed the quiet and peace of the place.

Barkwood, Shimmer, Vega and Kos searched the canopy of the immense forest for the mysterious owl, but he was nowhere to be found. Bawson, Crag and Hotchi scouted below. The tall straight trees stood silent and mystical, as if watching the progress of the visitors. The undergrowth sprouted taller than either fox or badger. Sacer sat high up on one of the mighty trees, keeping a sharp lookout. Crag could pick up many scents and tracks across the soft forest floor and there were well-established paths and runs through the scrub. But still they could see no evidence of the wise owl.

Hotchi found a cone by a tree stump. It had been stripped of its scales and the seeds were half chewed. Bawson sniffed it. 'Squirrel has been here not too long ago.'

'I was about to say that.' Hotchi was miffed.

'Oh sorry,' said Bawson. 'But I think Crag had already noticed it.'

'Look! See. A large pellet. That can mean only one thing. The owl was here.' Hotchi was overjoyed to be first with the news.

'Well done,' said Crag.

Sacer gave an alarm call to alert them. They wondered what the falcon had discovered. They couldn't see Barkwood, Vega or Shimmer. Kos could be clearly seen, sitting in a beech tree, but his attention seemed to be held by something beyond their vision.

'Can you see anything?' asked the hedgehog.

'Quiet, good friend,' said Crag.

Something moved stealthily through the thicket. There was definitely a creature behind the twisted and bent lichen-covered hawthorn. Hotchi quaked behind Crag. Bawson wanted to make a run for it.

Then out of the undergrowth burst a red deer. Bawson fell back, shaking.

'Welcome,' said the noble deer. 'I am Regal, the guardian of the forest. We have been expecting you.'

Kos swooped down on noiseless wings. Sacer followed. Barkwood, Vega and Shimmer landed on a fallen tree.

The deer addressed the little group: 'You wish to meet with Hibou, the wise owl. Well, he has agreed to see you. There is safe shelter in this forest for all benign travellers.'

'I knew there were deer here,' said Hotchi. 'I noticed the neat double prints in the soft earth.'

'Follow me,' said the tall red creature with the big wide eyes and twelve-pointed antlers.

The sun had sunk behind the trees. They could hear the bubbling song of a blackcap as they moved down the green aisles, following the deer who bounded gracefully through the forest. The birds flitted in and out among the ash, oak, elm, birch and beech. The hedgehog plodded on after them, trying to follow Crag's swinging brush; he knew he would not get lost as long as he could see that. Bawson sniffed the sweet airs of evening.

'He lives in the sunset tree,' said the deer, slowing down and picking his way through the brambles.

There was an air of expectancy as large wondering eyes stared and searched for the great owl. 'We wait here,' the deer instructed. They crouched, waiting and listening. The forest glade was silent and seemed deserted. The evening was balmy and warm.

Sacer scanned the still unexplored places. What secrets were hidden here? She sat brooding and wondering. The feeling were somehow akin to what she felt when she stayed with the ravens on the Sacred Cliffs.

The rich yellow light was gone, and the evening shadows had moved in. They were all aware of a special quality in the silence.

'Why is it called the sunset tree?' asked Vega, breaking the silence.

The deer looked at the kestrel. 'Long years ago ...' his mind seemed to leaf through the pages of time, 'the owls were the keepers of the Sacred Feather ... It was hidden in the hollow trunk and each evening it would glow. The tree would light up like the sun. Soon the oak got the name the sunset tree.'

They had all witnessed the beauty and power of the Sacred Feather. Now, finding the base of the mighty oak, their eyes followed slowly up along the biggest and oldest tree in the forest. Despite its partly hollow trunk, it had a massive canopy. Above the forest, stars pierced the velvet sky. A faint breeze ran through the leaves where ivy climbed to the first fork of the tree. A hole was clearly visible. The outline of an owl's head could just be discerned in the opening. As they gazed in wonder and awe he peered down at them, then slowly moved out on to the bough, ruffled his feathers, stretched his wings and flexed his claws.

The ancient eagle owl wore a solemn look as, opening his massive wings, he swooped down and alighted on a hollow log.

'I am Hibou, the keeper of the forest,' he declared.

CHAPTER 17

Words of Wisdom

A hare raised itself on to its hind legs, front paws dangling loose, and sat beside Bawson. A woodcock, with plumage that matched the forest floor, sat close to Hotchi the hedgehog. Barkwood was sitting with four long-eared owls. Kos watched a pair of barn owls sitting close together in an elm, his thoughts journeying back to Crannóg and Snowdrop, imagining the tender devotion they would be showering on the owlets.

Rabbits hopped among the ferns. The red deer sat on the soft spongy forest floor.

Crag was pleased to have discovered that his old friend Kuick the nightjar had found a home here in the bracken, along with a beautiful mate. A successful breeding season would mean they could fly home to Africa with pride and confidence.

Hotchi watched as a family of hedgehogs moved out to the clearing from a temple of leaves. The more richly-coloured tree sparrows sat with some house sparrows.

All the songsters had stayed awake to hear what the wise owl had to say. He seldom spoke but when he did it was always worth listening to.

Woodpigeons, stock doves, collared doves, even a pair of turtle doves sat in a yew tree. The thrush families, blackbird, robin, song and mistle, huddled together beside finches, linnets and yellowhammers. The tit families were well represented – coal, blue, great, long-tailed. Wagtails and all the summer visitors were there – chiff chaffs, willow warblers, white throats, wheatears and many more.

The place was alive with the forest dwellers. Squirrels, stoats, otters and fallow deer, were all present and waiting. Rooks and jackdaws sat proudly with Shimmer. They were elated to meet such a distinguished crow. Sacer did not see any peregrines, but there was no shortage of kestrels and sparrowhawks, all sitting with Vega. Pheasants and partridge were represented also in among the ferns, as were frogs, lizards and other small creatures.

The owl, with ear-tufts pricked up and wide staring eyes, asked the visitors to explain their plight.

Crag was about to speak when a beautiful young

vixen padded out and came near to him. She gently eased herself down beside him, gazed warmly at him with amber eyes, and swished her tail.

As Bawson watched, a sow badger emerged from under the roots of another oak. She sniffed the air and sidled over to Bawson. Bawson's head turned limply to one side. She nudged him gently.

'I'm called Moonlight,' she whispered tenderly. 'What's your name?'

'Bawson,' he replied a little self-consciously.

Hibou, the ancient owl, was very still, with only his eyes moving. 'Sit everyone, and listen,' he commanded.

Crag then explained the various misfortunes that had befallen them in such a short space of time, losing families and friends. He outlined the deaths in the falconry, the gassing of the Straffan clan of badgers, Kos losing his dear brother.

The fox related the trouble they had had with the rats. How the ancient site of Ratland was now being used again. Of the unusually large number of rats that had come from afar and seemed moulded by evil, and who had even organised the local rodents into an uprising against all other creatures.

He sounded the names of Fericul and Natas. Of course, he said, they were dead now, but he felt their evil ways had rubbed off on the present generation of rodents.

Bawson added that he himself was gifted with dreams, mostly troubled ones. As he explained some of them the other wildfolk listened attentively, and trembled at his words.

Shimmer then spoke, emphasising how they felt there was a definite connection between what was happening to them and the latest rat problem. He couldn't explain it, he just had a hunch that both were connected.

The old owl's eyes stared, deep and knowing.

'Even our sleep has been flooded with fear and anxiety,' exclaimed Bawson.

Hibou's eyes turned dark with troubled thoughts. Then he spoke: 'I've seen many things in my lifetime. I've been privileged to see great joys and wonders.

'Visions come to me in the night when the wise ones talk with me in the silence. The ancient forest dwellers gather around in the shadows to advise and support.' The moon illuminated his face. 'The wise ones tell me it is the Nusham we must fear. They are the most dangerous creatures on earth.'

The wildfolk sat, totally engrossed.

'The Nusham have brought mass death and destruc-tion upon the world. We must not let terror replace beauty.' His voice weakened.

'The machineries of death created by the Nusham give them this monstrous power. The shadow of destruction has fallen across the world, deepening and darkening day by day. Have we not enough problems with disease and other natural disasters – even death, which is beyond our control? Why should Nusham create new ways of inflicting hurt, pain, and suffering just because we're different from them?

'Even the rats you mentioned – Fericul and Natas. They were conceived by the Nusham.'

Bawson and Crag sat spellbound.

'We're all too aware of the dark details of Nusham crimes against nature,' Hibou continued. 'Our kind have witnessed many images of cruelty – animals and birds being torn apart by the blast of the death guns. The Nusham have a history of death and destruction. With their death technologies they want to crush the world like a flower.

'This mass desecration cannot be allowed any longer. The wildfolk have an ancient lineage, whereas the Nusham are not so long on the earth. They've a lot to learn. Yet in my travels I've seen many things, the two sides of the Nusham. I've seen the good Nusham doing kind things and healing the scars that others have made – planting trees, where the tree robbers had been, for example.

'But most of the Nusham have not taken to heart the message of nature. Instead they've made a black storm because of their evil thoughts and it will ravage the earth, destroying all in its way. This is the storm which tears down trees, pulls up soil, gouges holes in the earth, attacks rivers, lakes and seas, even the air. We must not go down before this storm. We must calm it, replace darkness with light. Let's sing to the time when the earth was clean and beautiful. Let's heal it again.'

All the song birds burst into most beautiful music and the words of the wise owl echoed through it.

'Let's change hate to understanding and kindness. Warfare and destruction – let it end. We must awaken all to peace and friendship. Let the Nusham hear our cries. Let there be awareness and unity. May the Nusham pull down their walls of petty misunderstanding, prejudices and hates of the past, for it is written in the *Sacred Book of Ravens*:

> "One day the hate will fall away from the Nusham as ice melts before the sun.

> "Then the spirit of love will arise, spreading over the earth, and we shall all bask in the glorious light of friendship."'

In the following silence each one pondered these thoughts.

'I think our weary travellers should rest now,' said the old owl as he shifted his body. Regal the red deer rose to his feet, and the animals of the forest slowly departed into the undergrowth and headed for their homes. The owl flapped up to his roost in the gnarled oak.

'Rest well,' said the red deer as he trotted away.

Moonlight nudged Bawson gently: 'Rest in my sett. It's secure under the protecting roots of the oak.'

Bawson sniffed the air as drops of rain began to patter on the leaves.

'You come too,' Moonlight said to Crag, 'and the hedgehog.'

'Hotchiwichi is my name, but you can call me Hotchi.'

'Your other friends will shelter well in the trees,' said Moonlight. 'You must all be paw-tired and weary-winged.'

The vixen, who was called Speedwell, cuddled up to Crag. 'Moonlight and I haven't lived here long, only since primrose time.'

'Do you have partners?' asked Crag.

Her eyes moistened. 'Mine was taken down by the death gun one winter, when we lived in the small woods. It was there I met Moonlight. Her mate was killed by the Nusham slave-dogs, the terriers.'

'Our sett is a fortress,' said Moonlight, trying to conceal her grief. Bawson's broad black muzzle twitched sadly. She snuggled up to him. 'Come on,' she whispered gently. They went down the sweet-smelling sett.

'It's a cunningly-designed sett,' said Speedwell the vixen. 'Don't you agree?'

'Yes,' said Crag and Bawson in unison.

Moonlight showed her embarrassment.

'Moonlight dug out every inch of it,' continued Speedwell. 'The curved passageways, with upper galleries for sleeping, the lower passages for feeding and play.'

'There's room for expansion, too,' said Moonlight, 'if there was a family here ...' She licked her bluish-grey fur. 'I've gathered dry bracken for you here. Rest well.'

Moonlight and Speedwell headed for the upper chambers.

'I suppose all the songbirds have their heads tucked in. Maybe the dawn chorus will be later than usual today,' chuckled Hotchi, looking around and expecting a response. But no response came. Crag, tail curled around his face, lay warm and snug, sound asleep. Bawson was also oblivious, snoring contentedly.

'That was quick,' grumbled the hedgehog. 'Here I am talking to myself.' He then curled up safely under the warm bracken.

CHAPTER 18

Old Legends Revealed

Bawson yawned, stretched and scratched, then with blinking eyes greeted the morning sunlight pouring down into the sett. Crag and Speedwell were already outside, looking at the majestic trees with their gracefully pendulous boughs, towering branches and thick canopy of leaves. The wrens and blue tits were hunting in the leaves for caterpillars. A tree creeper searched the rough-barked trunk for grubs or earwigs.

'A morning of stillness and splendour,' said Crag as he greeted Bawson.

'Oh, yes, very true.'

Moonlight had been collecting fresh dry bracken and grasses. She gave Bawson a friendly glance and moved backwards down the sett, hugging the bundles of bracken to herself. 'Back in a moment,' she smiled.

'A fine mate for some young boar,' commented Bawson.

'Or not so young,' said Speedwell teasingly.

Butterflies flitted along the rough track. A tortoiseshell basked on a sun-baked patch of fern. A jay searched for acorns through the thick dark foliage. Hotchi emerged from the sett. Above him Sacer, Shimmer and Vega sat in among the branches of the massive oak. Barkwood continued to sleep soundly in an old raven's nest.

A gentle footfall creeping softly in the stillness heralded the appearance of Regal, the red deer. 'I hope you've rested well. Hibou has requested a meeting. With the travellers only,' he added.

Crag rose to his feet, had a long stretch and yawned. Bawson looked at Moonlight. 'Something for our ears only, I'm afraid.'

Moonlight licked him behind the ear. The old badger pulled away shyly.

Speedwell spoke: 'We shall meet later, dear Crag.' She brushed along his body.

Hotchi looked at Crag and Bawson: 'Is it a pair of turtle doves I have for friends?' he teased.

The red deer looked to the trees. The birds were ready. Kos, who was resting above the ravens' nest, nudged Barkwood awake. They set out through the green glade, surprised that the great owl wanted to see them so quickly.

'It must be very urgent,' said Regal as he led the way into the heart of the forest.

Up ahead they could see a clearing with a crystal pool that mirrored the surrounding trees, while a chorus of birds warbled their songs. Flies were jigging up and down in the shade. The red deer moved softly, gently brushing the ferns as he made his way towards the pool. He beckoned the others forward. The birds flitted above, Shimmer's plumage shining like metal in the sun.

Suddenly they saw the great owl as he floated through the green glade and over the water, to land on a tree trunk that lay prostrate on the forest floor.

'Come, join me,' commanded the old owl. Sacer, Kos, Shimmer and Barkwood all perched on the same trunk. Crag, Bawson and Hotchi sat on the soft grasses. The deer stood still as a tree. An acorn dropped from the thick notched leaves. The owl swivelled his head as he peered at the helmeted acorn.

'Nothing escapes my ears,' he said in a warm voice. He sat motionless. 'You've rested well, I take it.'

They nodded back.

'Good.' Then his expression became anxious as he gave a backward glance.

'My father used to say the Nusham have gone mad; only nature remains sane. I'm over twenty summers in this splendid forest. How life has flowed by.' His eyes sparkled and flashed as he remembered. 'My old body is tired, but my mind is certainly not.'

Looking to the young birds he spoke caringly: 'You must never miss a chance to learn from others. While you develop your bodies you must not neglect your minds. It's the mind, not strength of body, that leads us to wisdom.' After a pause he continued: 'I asked you all here because there was something I didn't speak about last evening.'

The friends cocked their ears, eager to listen.

'What is it?' Hotchi pressed the owl.

'I reflected on Bawson's dreams,' the owl replied. 'I feared the worst but tried not to believe it, for it is now legend, eons old.'

'What?' asked Kos.

Hibou, the wise owl, spoke slowly: 'Long ago,

when the world was young, it was united by love and knowledge. A rodent named Laab, who was very strong, lived for a time on the Sacred Cliffs.

'He became envious of the ravens because they had the gift of scribing. But he was too proud to ask them to teach him. One night he had a wicked thought, and from this thought grew many more evil ideas.

'He planned to steal the Sacred Feather of Light and the *Sacred Book of Ravens*, the latter shortly to be completed by the scribes. He persuaded others to join with him. He would have his own kingdom in Ratland. Seasons passed as he worked on his dark deeds.

'He spawned the malice race and they lived secure in the bowels of the earth. Then, when the time was ripe, he and his legions set to work. They attacked the Council of Ravens, killing all but one. Laab then used the power of the Eagle of Light to pierce a deep hole in the ground; this would be the site for Ratland. He had secured the Sacred Feather and the *Sacred Book*. He was the supreme ruler.

'He planned to steal the colours of day, shut up light and leave only darkness. He then had an idea that with the power of the Sacred Feather he could turn his own claw into a magic claw. But the power of the Feather was given only for good. Laab's claw turned to magic but it was grotesque, black as night, just like his heart.

'The eagles of Mount Eagle and my ancestors from

these parts came and searched out the hordes of malice. A fierce and terrible battle took place. The Sacred Feather was finally recaptured as was the *Sacred Book*.

'Laab, clutching his withered claw which had been severed in the battle, escaped with some of his followers down the tunnel of darkness. The surviving members of the Council of Ravens sealed the hole with the power of the Feather. I fear the rats have indeed found this wicked Claw,' sighed Hibou.

They sat for a time in silence, Shimmer reflecting on the time he discovered the Sacred Feather hidden in the great elm.

'If this is true, if somehow the rats have discovered the Claw with its dark powers, what can be done?' asked Barkwood.

'We're willing to risk our all to destroy this thing,' declared Kos.

The great owl ruffled his feathers: 'You are brave and of good heart. You've even journeyed to Rat-land in the past. But if the rats have this power the consequences are too terrible to imagine. It is said that Laab and his hordes, sometimes called the Spoilers or haters of the light, were the ones who planted the seeds of darkness into the minds of the Nusham when they were young on the earth.'

'No creature will be safe,' mused Bawson, 'if they're allowed to use this evil object.'

'It must be located somewhere in Ratland,' said Crag. 'We'll just have to return to that vile place and destroy it.'

The great owl sighed sadly: 'No doubt it is in Ratland, but in the lower regions of that grim place. I fear that if any enter there they'll lose not only life, but spirit also ...'

'We're still prepared to take that risk,' said Vega, 'For the sake of the many.'

The owl's eyes misted over.

'What is the way?' asked Crag.

'Light must replace darkness. That's the only way,' said Hibou. 'But beware if you attempt to journey into the dark regions. All your senses will be assailed with the worst terrors you can imagine. It's the most feared place of all.'

'There is no time to delay,' said Sacer, 'now that we know what must be done.'

'This forest and its wildfolk will always welcome you back here,' said Regal, the red deer, gently.

'Thank you for that,' Crag smiled.

'I'll leave you all now,' said the old owl. 'If you succeed, and I sincerely hope you do, for all our sakes, you'll find me in the sunset tree. This is, if the Grey Owl hasn't called me away. Let me leave you with this prayer:

"May the Eagle of Light send health,
strength and victory to you
and may you pad and fly the forest
for many seasons to come.'"

With that, Hibou stretched his wings and flapped away high over the tall trees.

'I'll escort you to the edge of the woods,' offered the red deer. 'And if you wish I'll raise a band of helpers to assist you in your mission.'

'No, thank you,' said Crag. 'It's best we go ourselves.'

As they passed by the majestic giants they could hear the metallic twittering of blue tits.

'It'd be nice to watch the passage of seasons through this great forest,' said Crag.

'The tender days of spring,' said Hotchi.

'The song of the summer songsters,' added Bawson.

'The fiery colourful autumn,' said Hotchi.

'The call of a vixen on a winter's night,' said Crag.

Moonlight was busy pawing the ground around some roots, the dark earth and leaves flying in the air, scooped up by her powerful, curved paws. Then she came towards Bawson and the others, and presented them with honey from a bees' nest.

'This'll help keep your strength up,' she said tenderly, knowing that they must leave.

The kestrels and hawks shared their secret larder

with Barkwood, Vega, Kos, Shimmer and Sacer, while below Crag, Hotchi and Bawson gorged themselves on the delicious honey.

There was a sadness in the air as they said farewell to the wildfolk of the great forest. Speedwell licked Crag's face several times and moved up and down his body, scenting him. Her young eyes, full of summer, stared at Crag and she said she'd wait for him.

'Let's go,' said the hedgehog.

Moonlight nuzzled Bawson: 'Remember me ...'

Bawson turned awkwardly away and thanked the red deer. 'Farewell!' said the others, as they edged their way out into the fields.

Sacer, Kos, Barkwood, Vega and Shimmer wheeled and circled in the air.

'Don't get lost,' said Crag to the hedgehog, turning for a last look back at Speedwell.

'I'll stay right behind you, turtle dove,' teased Hotchi.

CHAPTER 19

Crusade of Hate

'Traitor!' snarled a voice. Spook awoke with a start, then trembled at the sight of the sick green fog permeating his sleeping chambers. Hack stirred and nudged Spike. The sinister red eyes and black form of Laab were clearly visible. Other rats scurried off down the passageways.

'You've lost the desire for revenge,' the voice of Laab hissed from the fog.

'No!' said Spook, grovelling.

'Did you not swear to carry on the warfare until all rodents' enemies were destroyed?'

'Yes. Every last one,' squealed Spook.

'I hope you're not trying to thwart my plan.'

'No, your Excellency, your Highness.'

'Don't try to lie to me,' hissed Laab. 'I can smell lies

a mile away. Remember it was I who created them. While you orgy on food and sleep, your enemies are gathering. They've been getting information about our secret weapon.'

The rats recoiled.

'They're coming here!' Laab continued. 'The falcon from the Sacred Cliffs lives, and is with them.'

'Impossible,' cried Hack.

'Don't dare argue with me or you might be minus your other eye,' Laab threatened.

Hack ducked down behind Spike.

'We are at this moment planning a counter attack,' said Spike.

'You,' Spook turned to Spike. 'Send out a thousand of our best fighting rats. Tell them to lay an ambush. No enemy must ever defile this Kingdom again. Go to it!' Spike scurried away as quickly as he could.

'Spook, you're a sly lying trickster, but I admire those qualities.' Laab then broke into a snarling rage. 'I gave you a special gift. I expect it to be used, not left lying idle for days. Watch me summon the power.' The green light swirled round and round as he moved his claw over the Claw of Darkness.

'I had to forfeit a great deal for this power,' Laab declared. They could see the pool of enchantment forming. 'Now use it!' demanded Laab.

Spook's white fur stood on end. He wanted to impress this spectre, but how? He knew the rats would easily kill their enemies. Something more impressive. 'Yes!' he yelled. 'I have it. A Nusham. One that has laid down poison to kill us. He will now die.'

'Easy on,' said Hack.

With that a farmer could be seen walking across his field. 'Move along, Spartacus,' he nudged an animal ahead of him. 'Time I had my dinner.' The bull advanced slowly to gentle prods of the stick. The farmer then went ahead to open the gate. As he did so, a change suddenly came over the gentle giant. His eyes flashed red and menacing.

'What is it, fella?' said the farmer. 'My god!' the man cried as he looked into the bull's eyes. The bull charged.

'No ... ' The pool faded.

'Good!' said Laab. His red eyes widened in sheer delight. 'I'll return soon to check on you again, so be warned.' Then he faded into the mist.

'What a loathsome creature,' said Hack. 'Why can't he do his own evil work?'

'Dear Hack, I wish I were back in the cage at the laboratory. Life was so much simpler then.' Spook sounded very weary now.

'It would be wonderful to live the life of a normal rat, foraging in the cities with my mates, instead of all this warfare,' sighed Hack.

'We're in too deeply to turn back now,' said Spook.

Just then Whizzer the crow came along.

'The falcon was *not* killed,' snapped Spook. The

hooded crow looked in disbelief. 'She's still alive,' the King continued. 'You'll have to try again and don't fail this time. If you do we'll all suffer.'

'I'll go now,' said Whizzer. 'And I'll bring back a primary feather just to prove she's dead.'

'No need to go just yet,' said Spook. 'Let's eat first. Then you can depart.'

Spike joined them for breakfast. 'A thousand of our best fighting rats have just left,' he reported. 'They'll attack our enemies long before they ever reach Ratland.'

*   *   *

Bawson seemed very nervy as they passed the fens. A wood pigeon lifted off from a hazel and flapped away in alarm. A chill wind blew.

Something's not quite right, thought Crag.

Vega suddenly gave out an alarmed *kee-kee-kee-kee*. From where he hung in the air he had caught sight of a huge horde of rats.

'Rats?' Terror gripped Bawson.

Crag nodded.

The sleek rats slid like snakes through the wet grasses. Sacer circled low, indicating where they were lying like flocks of demons, swarming from every corner of the grasses.

The rats sprang into the air. 'Attack! Attack!' they yelled. They scurried, squirming, bristling into action, leaping on to Bawson's back, biting at Crag's face, clamping their sharp incisors around Hotchi's legs.

Barkwood swooped down, piercing the life out of one rat. Kos locked his talons around another. Sacer raked their squirming bodies. Two rats climbed on to Kos, but Vega and Shimmer tore them away. Clawing, snapping, biting and tearing, the two groups faced each other in deadly combat.

Crag tried to shake away the hideous creatures, and he succeeded. Dozens fell dead but still more came. Screaming and squealing and wailing like sirens their bristling bodies leapt and fell.

Bawson snapped and lashed out with his powerful claws, sending many crashing to their deaths. Shimmer hammered their heads with his pick-like bill. The owls and falcons raked and tore but still more rodents leapt and bit with their razor-sharp teeth.

All seemed lost as the rats continued to attack, when suddenly the friends heard the harsh call of Sheila the heron. Dark looming shadows passed overhead and in an instant, in wheeling circles, the great birds descended – Sheila with the black vulture and the bateleur eagle from the falconry. They swooped down with powerful claws and sharp beaks. They kicked and clawed the rats, delivering lethal blows to many. More help was on its way: Shimmer could hear rooks emitting their heavy cries as they glided over the fields and swarmed down.

The rats kept on darting, scrabbling, teeming every-where. Hordes of them fell, blood spurting from muzzles, heaving masses squealing and writhing, jaws snapping in a desperate attempt to mount a final attack. The arrival of the rook colonies, however, sealed their fate. The rats crashed down in twisting heaps. Soon the lifeless forms of a thousand rats lay torn and scattered in the grasses.

Shimmer was profoundly relieved to see all his clan. 'You came in the nick of time,' he said.

'Thanks to Sheila,' said one rook, 'she always has her ear to the ground.'

Looking at Sacer, Sheila said proudly: 'I told you, I know everything that goes on around here.'

Vega and Kos were delighted to see the black vulture and the bateleur eagle finally free from the falconry.

Crag panted and licked his wounds, then sank down on all fours. 'I'm getting too old for all this fighting,' he sighed. He had small bites on his hind legs, flank and belly with blood running freely from them and he also had deep gashes on his face.

Bawson compared wounds with him.

Barkwood and Vega had received serious injuries to their wings and legs. Hotchi was limping badly. Sacer, Shimmer and Kos had only minor cuts.

'Well, we're all still in one piece,' said a relieved Crag. The wind deepened across the open country.

'Let's take shelter in that old barn away from Nusham eyes,' suggested Shimmer. He thanked all the rooks and dismissed them. They flew off in a clatter, cawing in triumph. The small group then eased their way over to the abandoned barn.

Crag sated his thirst from a nearby rainwater pool.

'Those snarling vicious brutes,' growled Bawson. 'Will they never learn?'

'Rest yourself, old friend,' said Crag, his body aching with hurt and fatigue. 'Thank you, friends, for coming to our aid,' he said to the black vulture and the bateleur eagle.

Exhaustion finally overtook them all and they slept soundly.

CHAPTER 20

Uneasy Alliance

Shrugging off his sleepiness, Crag stretched and licked his wounds. His fur was matted with dried blood which he now tried to clean.

Before the hour of dawn Sacer and Kos had flown to the scene of the battle and brought back many rat corpses to store in the barn; they would all need to eat later.

Bawson jolted into sudden wakefulness, wondering whether he had just dreamt that terrible episode with the rats. His aching body made him all too conscious that he had not.

Hotchi was still asleep. Barkwood was awake but, like Vega, was feeling very poorly. Shimmer was washing his throbbing leg in cool rainwater. The black vulture and bateleur eagle crouched on a beam, still trying to get used to the idea of being free to fly any place they might choose. Sheila stood meticulously preening her feathers, then she flapped and shook the drowsiness from her wings.

Sacer sat high on a beam beside the opening, her face turned towards the sky. She thought long and hard. 'You must replace darkness with light.' That was what the old owl had told them. That's also what the *Book of Ravens* teaches but how could they achieve that? Sacer pondered the question for a while. Then, struck by a flash of inspiration, she turned to Crag.

'I know how we can combat the Claw of Darkness,' she declared.

The others stirred and paid careful attention. The fox trotted over and looked up at the falcon.

'How?' he asked eagerly.

'The Sacred Feather. It's more powerful than any other magic. Its light will banish the darkness,' said Sacer.

'It's a wonderful idea,' mused Crag in a low voice. 'But I don't think the Council of Ravens would dare risk losing such a precious object. And that's what could easily happen. No, I don't think they'd risk it.'

'We could ask them,' said Sacer, dropping down to the ground beside Crag.

'But do you think they really have this Claw of Darkness?' the hedgehog asked no one in particular.

They all looked at him in dismay.

'Yes, I suppose they do,' he sighed.

'If I leave now and don't rest I could be at the Sacred Cliffs before sunset,' said Sacer.

'That would be splendid,' said Crag. 'If you can convince them that all life is at risk now that the rats have this deadly weapon.'

'I'll go with you,' suggested Shimmer.

'I'd certainly like the company,' said Sacer.

'We wish you luck,' said Bawson in farewell.

Sacer and Shimmer then took to their wings and sped away across the grey skies.

'We'll wait until nightfall before we head for Ratland,' said Crag, after the two birds had flown out of sight. 'By then they should have arrived at the Sacred Cliffs, all being well, and will have the Sacred Feather at Ratland before first light.'

'It all sounds far too easy,' said the battle-weary badger. 'But the reality is usually far from easy.'

'Let's eat,' said Crag.

The escapees from the falconry were asked about the trouble there. Kos and Vega remembered the place with a mixture of joy and sadness as they listened to the black vulture relating the story of its last sorry days – how the dogs went berserk killing the birds, green froth drooling from their mouths. 'It was horrible,' sighed the vulture.

Bawson shuddered. 'They must've been under the spell of the Claw of Darkness. I'm convinced that's it.'

'What reason would the rats have for destroying us?' asked the bateleur eagle.

'Those who destroy and kill don't need reasons,' snapped the badger.

'Well, some good can come out of even the most terrible deeds,' said Barkwood. They looked at him in surprise. 'You two are free, who've been prisoners for years!'

'I can't believe it,' smiled the black vulture.

'What do you plan to do, now that you're free?' Kos asked them.

'Stay here for a time,' the eagle spoke for the two of them. 'Then, hopefully, when we're truly strong and fit, we'll fly the great flight to our homeland in Africa. We're a bit unsure about how to get there, but we'll risk the journey someday.'

'Not intending to alarm you or anything, but it'll be very difficult to conceal your presence around here,' said Hotchi. 'Nobody expects to see a vulture or an eagle when they look up in the sky. The Nusham would probably try to shoot you just because you're there–'

Crag interrupted the hedgehog: 'The skies of Africa were made for the eagle and vulture,' he said. 'There they can soar high over the great mountain peaks and glide across wide savannahs. And while I don't actually know anything about Africa, a friend might, who lives in the great forest. A nightjar. He, I'm sure, would help you find your way there.' The vulture and the eagle looked very pleased at that possibility.

They swopped stories with Kos and Vega about the falconry. They recalled the birds who had tried to escape but failed; how Kos and Vega were like beacons of light to them all when they sat cold and damp, huddled on their blocks, knowing that at least two dear friends had found the freedom of the skies.

'So you two were the last to escape?' enquired Hotchi.

'We heard of a peregrine who got out through a window of the Nusham house the day we escaped, but he was never seen again,' said the black vulture.

They sat talking for most of the day. It took Crag's mind off the desperate journey he knew he must make at nightfall.

*   *   *

Outside in the distant fields Whizzer circled the fens and saw the carnage of battle. He alighted on the grass and walked among the cold, twisted, lifeless bodies. Over a thousand black and brown rats dead, and not one of their enemies slain!

He pecked and fed on the moist eyes. Then he lifted off the ground and hurried back to Ratland to report on the heavy losses.

Spook was visibly shaken when he heard the news the hooded crow had to relate – a whole regiment of his best troops wiped out!

Many of the rat families had left when the Claw of Darkness was first revealed. They'd wanted no part of it. Now more of the rats decided to leave. They fled back to the cities, to river banks, sewers and warehouses, all wanting to live like normal rats again. Mice, shrews and voles fled as well. Spook found his empire dwindling daily.

'When things are going well they all want to be here, but when things get bad they vanish like smoke,' he grumbled.

'We're still with you,' said Hack.

Spook blinked back some tears. 'I know. And I'm grateful for that. I have you, dear loyal subjects, and that.' He pointed to the Claw of Darkness.

'Why doesn't Laab himself use the power of the Claw?' asked Spike. They all looked at the passageway from which he'd entered.

'Maybe because he lives so far below ground that the magic doesn't work there,' suggested Hack.

'I doubt that,' said Spook. 'Maybe his attitude is: "why bark when you have a dog to do it".'

'You foolish rodents!' An old rat who was preparing to leave had overheard their conversation.

'What do you mean, speaking like that to your king?' snapped Spike.

'It's okay, Spike,' said Spook. 'Why do you think we're so foolish?' he asked the old rat.

'That thing there has brought nothing but trouble

to us,' the old rat replied, pointing to the Claw. 'There was a time, brief though it was, when we all lived peacefully and happily here. We took our chances foraging at night like any other creature. Most of us felt secure, and we were content, even proud, to have you as king. But you've let yourself be taken over by the power of this evil object. You'll lose everything, perhaps even your life. Mark my words. That vile thing has power only if it's used. And you're foolish enough to use it for greed and control. Did you not have enough before this thing was given to you? Get rid of it. That's my final advice to you.' With that the rat scurried away.

'I wouldn't worry about what a foolish old rat has to say,' said Whizzer, trying to console Spook.

'Everything he said made sense,' sighed Spook. 'That's the trouble. He's one of the elders from the west. Very wise clan. I'm sorry I never asked his advice before. I mightn't be in such a terrible state as I find myself now.'

*   *   *

Night drew its mantle of darkness across the land.

'It's time to go, dear friend,' said Crag, nudging Bawson, who was dozing.

'Oh yes,' said the badger.

'You still want to go?' asked the fox.

'My relations are all dead, and my home is polluted,'

sighed Bawson. 'I must go and see if we can destroy this wicked object.'

'We're all ready,' said the others.

Hotchi limped over.

'Dear Hotchi, I think you'll have to stay until that leg of yours gets better,' said Crag.

'But ...'

'No arguing, good friend. You need to rest for a couple of days,' insisted Crag. 'That goes for you too, Vega and Barkwood. Those wounds will never heal if you don't rest them. Bawson, Kos and myself will go now. Perhaps, dear friends,' said the fox to the eagle and the vulture, 'You might follow at dawn and keep a lookout for Sacer and Shimmer.'

'We'll be glad to. We're not much use at night flying,' said the black vulture.

'There's plenty of food here, thanks to Sacer and Kos, and lots of snails and slugs for your delicate palate, Hotchi,' teased Crag.

'Oh, be off with you,' was the hedgehog's reply. 'And do be careful. You're on a very dangerous mission and you've a perilous journey ahead. I don't wish to lose the only turtle doves in the area,' he chuckled.

'Sheila said she'll call in tomorrow and check up on you,' said Crag.

'We're not invalids,' retorted Hotchi. 'Checking up on us indeed,' he mumbled to himself.

There was a distant rumble of thunder as they left the old barn. Bawson sniffed the air nervously. Kos scouted ahead.

Sometime later another clap of thunder came, this time noisy and scary. Crag felt very anxious, but didn't want to show it. Thunder didn't bother him but the power of the Claw of Darkness did. The thunder became more insistent, rolling around in the sky. Then a flash of lightning momentarily illuminated the countryside and the rain started drumming down. Flash after flash of lightning followed more ear-splitting crashes of thunder. The fox and the badger ran as fast as they could across the wide meadow in the driving rain. Hurrying clouds passed over them. Bawson soon began cringing and cowering.

'Come on, Bawson,' Crag called. 'We can shelter along this hedgerow belt.'

Kos watched from the hedgerow where he was sheltering in a blackthorn. He saw his friends moving along the hazel and brambles where they found some shelter from the downpour. Gradually the thunder grew fainter, and the rain eased. Then it stopped altogether.

Bawson's moistened nose read the air: 'I think that's the last of it for the night,' he said hopefully. Kos looked totally bedraggled and began to preen. He didn't like the heavy rain, but the evening was warm so he would dry off soon.

'Let's go,' said Crag from the shadows of the hedge, and loped away across the fields. They had to pass over a wide road where beams of vivid light cut into the darkness. Cars rushed through the night, heedless of wildfolk. Many a poor creature met disaster under passing wheels. Tears welled up in Kos's eyes as he thought of Driad, his life snuffed out like a tiny spark.

* * *

After a time they reached a vast and dreary bog. A shifting grey fog hung low over the ground. Kos watched Crag slinking through the peaty ground, Bawson trundling beside him. This place made Kos nervous and he glanced over his shoulder several times.

Finally, they reached Ratland. They knew it from the stark, dead trees of the desolate place, and the barren tangle of briars covering the entrance to the passage tomb. The rats now used a different entrance, at the side. It was large enough for Bawson to walk through and he did. Kos followed Crag into the eerie place. It seemed silent as the grave. They'd expected to meet at least a couple of rodents on sentry duty but not one rat was to be seen. The fresh tracks seemed well-used but there was no sign of life.

They had not entered this passageway before, but expected it would lead to the main chambers. Bawson was relieved that he didn't have to pass the Nusham tombs. They really gave him the creeps.

Kos was busy removing earwigs from his white plumage. It really was like being on the edge of blackness, he thought to himself.

Then they came upon the wall of skulls which made them shudder with horror.

'What mind spawns a place like this?' asked the nervous badger. Rounding the next bend, they found themselves in a gallery. There were plenty of signs that rodents had been living in it, yet now it was quite deserted.

'Perhaps we've killed them all,' said Kos.

'I don't think so,' remarked a cautious Crag.

By now they had passed several galleries and tunnels, but still no rats.

'It's a relief,' whispered Bawson. 'I wouldn't care if I never saw one again.'

'Shush,' said Kos. 'I hear something.'

'What?' asked the badger, his heart pounding in his chest.

'Rats!' said Crag in a low voice. 'Just ahead in the next chamber.'

*   *   *

Spook sat upon his throne.

'We're quite alone,' he said to Hack, Spike and Whizzer. 'Not one of the rats has come back.'

'We should leave here before dawn, return to the

city dump and take our chances there. What do you say to that?' asked Hack.

'I think it's our best option,' agreed Spike.

'Maybe they're right,' said Whizzer. 'Just leave this place, and the Claw.'

'What if Laab comes after us? He could haunt us, or worse. Did any of you consider that? Well?' sniffed Spook.

He sniffed and sniffed. 'I smell fox,' he said, becoming suddenly alarmed. They turned quickly to find fox, badger and owl standing at each of the exits from the chamber.

'We meet again,' said Crag.

'Don't try to make a run for it,' growled Bawson, waving his powerful paw. 'Where is this Claw of Darkness?' he demanded.

'How do you know?'

'Never mind how we know. Where is it?' asked Crag.

'It's right there,' said Spook, pointing to the stone shrouded in green light. 'Take it. Have it as a present. We're done with it.'

'So this is the vile thing that has brought so much pain and death,' said Crag, inching over to it. 'Does it have a mind of its own?' he asked.

'Yes! No!' blurted Spook. 'What exactly do you mean?'

'Terrible things have been done with its power,' said Bawson.

'Agreed,' said Spook. 'Terrible, vile things.'

'Well, who used its power?' demanded Crag.

Spook trembled.

'Once you meddle with its magic it seems to take you over,' said Hack.

'That's it exactly,' pleaded Spook.

'It must be destroyed,' said Kos.

'Impossible, I believe,' said Spook.

'Impossible? Then it must be returned to where it came from,' said Kos.

'That's easy,' Spook sniggered nervously. 'It came from down there,' pointing to a strange doorway in the next chamber.

'Well, we'll have to return it,' declared Crag.

'Take it,' said Spook. 'No one will prevent you.'

'We shall all return it,' insisted Crag.

'No! That's not a very good idea,' cried Spook nervously.

'Are we to expect an ambush like yesterday?' asked an angry Bawson.

'No,' said Spook. 'The battle is over, I mean, the war. You're the victors. You'll have no trouble from us again. That's a promise from a king.'

'Well, since we're such friends,' said Crag, 'you won't mind coming with us, down to the lower regions with the Claw.'

'We have been down there once,' said Spike, 'and have no wish to go there ever again.'

'Help us or die!' declared Bawson bluntly.

'Well, since you put it like that, how can we refuse?' said the hooded crow. With that he made a bolt for it and escaped up one of the tunnels.

'Will I go after him?' asked Kos.

'No,' said Crag. 'I think we'll need all the help we have right here.' They stood very still. It was decision time. They looked long and silently at the entrance.

'It looks sinister,' said Bawson. 'It's probably fraught with danger.'

'Maybe we should just bury the Claw and leave,' suggested Spook. His words fell on deaf ears.

Kos flapped over and clasped the evil claw with his sharp talons. 'I'll carry it.'

'Please. I don't want to go,' pleaded Spook. 'Laab once said: "No one returns from this place alive."'

'Who's Laab?' asked Kos.

'You'll find out soon enough if you go down there,' said Hack.

'Let's go,' said Crag, as he stepped into the blackness.

CHAPTER 21

Journey into Darkness

Into the throes of darkness they journeyed, Kos leading the way, flapping slowly ahead and holding the vile Claw, its green light illuminating the darkness as they descended lower and lower. Bawson stayed at the rear just in case the rats should try to make a getaway. It was a journey into the abyss, and they didn't know when it would end or what they would find.

As they made their long, slow descent, they passed through corridors of gloom whose tortured walls seemed to scream silently back at them. It became more nightmarish with each step. There appeared to be vast reaches of emptiness ahead of them. Was this a plan, Crag wondered, to draw them into the enchantment of darkness, that they should be lost forever? He shuddered at the thought.

Trying to maintain a calm expression, he glanced back at the terrified rats moving with quick, jerky actions behind him. A dripping sound teased the strange stillness. The further they travelled the more oppressive it all became.

Bawson thought he heard whispers, evil, loathsome whispers. His eyes bulged in his head. The black now seemed a grey nothingness. Grey stones, sharp and petrified, partially lined the way. Strange gloomy smells assaulted their nostrils, making them feel ill.

'Think of something pleasant,' suggested Crag. 'Sweet summer flowers, a crystal-clear pool, the great forest ...'

Bawson began to think of Moonlight. She was so beautiful. Why had he been so stuffy and formal? He imagined a walk with her through the silver forest with only the moon for company. He remembered her gentle ways and sweet honeysuckle smell. Sadness engulfed him again. He couldn't hold on to the precious thoughts no matter how hard he tried.

'This is a hopeless task,' he sobbed. 'Let's return before it's too late.'

Crag moved back to comfort him. 'Easy, old pal. We came to do a job and we're going to finish it, come what may.'

'Sorry, dear Crag, it's this place ... not an ounce of joy in it.'

They struggled on down winding stone steps,

through mists of emptiness, and finally to a maze of dark corridors that seemed to be going nowhere.

'This monstrous grey is driving me mad,' moaned Bawson, his voice echoing in the emptiness. The web of passages offered no clues, and the grey void seemed to mock them.

Out of the nothingness the swirling grey began to change, and a vast pit, boiling and bubbling with green fluid, appeared before them, a plunging ravine on the left. One false step and they'd be gone.

'What a place,' whispered Crag, coming to a sudden halt. 'It's like being in the final blackness, from which all light and warmth are removed.'

'We're caught in some grotesque trap, if you want my opinion,' said Bawson. The bleak aura chilled the air. They felt ensnared, with no way out. On they moved, skirting the pit, scared and listless.

Kos was like a light in the darkness as he circled and flapped unfalteringly ahead.

Rounding the next bend they saw in the distance a lake of fire, the roar of the flames beckoning them forwards.

Terror gripped them as a ghastly verdant pallor overlaid the black and grey tones. The sick green light swirled about, swamping them, and there was a smell of decay in the lifeless air. Grim walls revealed another passageway. The heavy pungent

odour cloying
the air made
them gag. The
grimness of the
place threatened to
overcome their minds.

Bawson looked back at the tortured landscape of
butts and ravines. The whole place was haunted by
the spectre of evil.

Then a voice spoke:

'What a surprise! And such distinguished visitors at
that.' They quickly pinpointed where the voice was
pouring out from.

'Welcome. This is my humble abode,' hissed
Laab, his red eyes glowing in their black sockets.

'So you found the gateway to the underworld, with a little help from King Rat ...'

'They made me come here,' grovelled Spook.

'Silence!' ordered Laab. 'Enter. The barn owl has already arrived. He knows my friends well. I think you should be familiar with them too.'

Crag and Bawson entered, followed by Spook, Hack and Spike. All their worst nightmares were re-awakened then. There, alongside Laab, stood Fericul, Natas and Moloch.

'Salutations!' said Fericul and Natas in unison, their blood-red eyes glowering menacingly.

'They've come like moths to the flame,' hissed Laab.

CHAPTER 22

The Lightbearer

Sacer sat crouched outside the cave where the Council members were meeting, wild dark eyes displaying the tension she was feeling. Shimmer was inside, pleading the case on their behalf. The Council of Ravens looked very solemn. They wanted to help their friends, but if they should lose the Sacred Feather by allowing it to be taken to the pit of darkness, what would befall the animal kingdom?

'We were without the Feather for a long time and we've seen the suffering that took place without its protection,' said one elder.

'Maybe all the recent tragedies have been coincidences,' suggested another.

'Are we sure this Claw of Darkness really exists?' asked a third.

Shimmer could not truthfully say yes or no.

Granet was aware of the legend of the Claw of Darkness. 'If the rats have this weapon, they could turn our world into everlasting night' he said grimly.

'Let's vote on it,' said Corvus. 'And I think Shimmer should also be allowed to vote, since it was he who returned this treasured possession to the Sacred Cliffs.'

There was a hint of daybreak in the sky. Sacer thought of her companions and wondered whether they had gone to Ratland or were waiting for her to return. She guessed they would have gone anyway, help or no help. What if they were attacked? None of them was in a fit state to do any more fighting, although they had resolved to succeed or die. The waiting was unbearable.

Shimmer emerged with Granet and Corvus and beckoned Sacer inside. Granet spoke gravely to Sacer: 'Because of the great loyalty of your family to these Sacred Cliffs, and because of our dear friends who were prepared to risk their very lives to help the many, the Council have agreed to let you take the Sacred Feather to the pit of darkness.'

Sacer felt a great relief.

'Guard this sacred object with your life,' urged Granet. 'It must not fall into the wrong hands, and it must be returned as soon as possible to the Sacred Cliffs.'

Sacer readily agreed, thanking them profusely.

Corvus then brought out the beautiful feather. Its golden glow dazzled her.

'Remember,' said Corvus, 'its power must be used only for good.'

'Open your right wing,' said one of the ravens to Sacer. Sacer did so, and with his powerful bill the raven yanked out one of her primary feathers. Sacer flinched with pain, stifling a scream.

Her primary was carefully placed beside the large feather. The ravens then made a circle around the two feathers and stretched out their wings, until they overlapped with one another. Granet prayed for protection for Sacer and the success of her mission.

Then he whispered some strange crow language she could not understand. Suddenly circles of rainbow light pulsated from the Sacred Feather. As the falcon looked in awe, the feather began to shrink to the size of her own. The light was now a gentle candleglow.

Corvus took the Feather of Light and gently put it into Sacer's wing, exactly where her own had previously been. 'Go now in safety,' said Granet, 'and may the powers of light be with you.'

Sacer thanked them again and turned to go. She noticed that Shimmer's eyelids were drooping with sleep.

'You should rest,' she said softly. He protested, opening his eyes wide. 'Rest here and I'll return soon,' said Sacer.

Shimmer finally agreed. 'Take care, precious falcon,' he whispered warmly.

Sacer ruffled her feathers and, curving her crescent wings, lifted off over the rocks, flew past the gorse bushes, and slipped over the cliff ledge. Below, in the heavy swell of the sea, a procession of dark-winged shearwaters skimmed and wavered over the ocean. Sacer flew in a direct course. The ravens watched the brave falcon, her body hazed in the golden light.

A Nusham walked along the sheep's track that led up to the Cliffs. He held up the left collar of his jacket, shielding the cigarette he was lighting. Pulling hard on the cigarette, he noticed the falcon shape across the morning sky.

'I must tell Phil that falcon is back on the cliffs,' he muttered to the silence.

* * *

Kos could see rats teeming behind him in the shadows, moving silently like spectres. The walls were covered completely with the vile green fog and it shrouded the entrances.

'Did you notice the markings above the door as you entered?' asked Laab. 'Well, let me decipher them for you.' And he read: 'Let no one step beyond this door if he fears death.' Laab laughed, a cruel empty sound.

Bawson arched his body, ready to fight, his fur stiffened up to make him look twice his real size.

'There's no need to fight here,' sniggered Natas. 'We'd like to show you something.'

'We don't want to see,' snapped Bawson.

'Oh, you've no choice,' said Natas. 'You won't be able to close your eyes or fall asleep until you see how well the power of the Claw has been used. I'll show you pain within pain, misery within misery.

Kos shivered. Spook sat behind Crag. Try though they did they could not shut their eyes.

'Let the show begin,' said Fericul.

Faint images began to appear on all the green walls and in the distance the sound of terrible screaming and shrieking could be heard. Then the pictures became clearer. Their senses were assailed by the most frightening images.

'Here is a brief episode in the life of a dying planet,' shouted Laab, over the screams.

They gazed deeply, as if compelled, at the horrible images.

'The source of all your terrors, in front of your very eyes,' said Moloch.

Then began the glimpses of cruelty and destruction, misery and pain. The friends shrank down in horror as the pictures flashed past.

Burning and devastation, hideous massacres. Torture, beating, shooting. Bombing, gassing, spraying. Freezing and starvation. Their senses were pushed beyond the limits of endurance.

'Artists of cruelty. Plenty of technique, don't you think?' Laab's voice echoed with excitement.

They watched the wildfolk's endless trek through landscapes devastated by the Nusham. They watched timber thieves and other spoilers of the forest.

'Seen enough?' Natas's eyes gleamed red at Crag.

Screeches and screams of pain which no eardrums could endure, fires burning in forests consuming everything, charred trees, wildfolk fleeing the destruction. Nothing was spared. Mountains, trees, seas, rivers, land. Whirlwinds of dust and fire. Craters and veils of smoke. Big pounding guns, limbs blasted apart.

The mental poisoning continued, invading all of their senses with the deepest and darkest of nightmares. Wildfolk and Nusham were disappearing before their very eyes, felled by the death guns, trapped or torn down by machines. Bleached skulls lay all about on the scorched earth.

Now Kos could see his mother dangling from a post, the pole trap biting deep into her legs. Bawson witnessed badgers gasping in agony as gas choked the life out of them. Crag could see the hounds gaining on his mate Asrai and tearing her limb from limb; he could see his two offspring strangled by hedgetraps.

The friends lay down silently, shattered by sorrow. The images gone, they could finally close their eyes. Tears flowed uncontrollably. Hack, Spike and Spook sat stunned and silent.

Crag thought of the old owl's question: 'Must terror replace beauty?' It seemed so. He lay on his side, eyes tightly shut, feeling life ebb away.

'I'm afraid we've murdered their minds,' said Laab to the other demons in mock sadness.

* * *

Crag gradually became aware of the exquisite fragrances of wild flowers and grasses wafting to his nostrils. It was the sweet smell of meadows and hedgerows. The most important need in his whole being was to sniff those scents. There it was again, closer, stronger. He could identify them all, white and pink clovers, meadow-sweet vernal grass, eglantine. The air filled with the delicate scents.

Then a voice spoke: 'Wake up, dear friend. Wake up, please.'

The fox slowly opened his eyes. Everything was blurred at first, then he could see his dear friend the hedgehog, trying to remove bits of grass and clover from his prickly spines.

'What a dreary place,' said Hotchi. 'So gloomy. We nearly got lost several times. Only for that green mist we'd never have found you.'

'It's so good to see you,' said Crag. 'And smell you.'

'No one ever said that to me before,' said the hedgehog.

Barkwood nudged Kos awake. 'All right?' he asked

gently. Kos was well pleased to see the long-eared owl but noticed that Barkwood's cuts and lacerations were still torn and bloodied.

'You shouldn't have come,' said an anxious Kos.

'Oh, I've had worse,' said Barkwood. 'Besides, we were worried about you all.'

Spike, Hack and Spook awoke. They were just as pleased to see the new arrivals as the friends were. It seemed comforting.

Bawson thought the voices of his friends were but dreams, tricks of the mind. When he finally came to he could see Barkwood, Vega and Hotchi, the bateleur eagle and the black vulture alongside Crag and Kos.

'Sheila the heron is keeping vigil for Sacer. But there's no sign of her or Shimmer,' said Barkwood.

'I hope nothing went wrong,' said Bawson gravely.

'Let's get out of this vile place,' said Crag.

'There's gratitude,' said a voice from behind.

They trembled, for there was Laab once more, holding the Claw of Darkness, flanked by Fericul, Natas and Moloch.

'This can't be real,' said Vega.

'Oh, but it is,' hissed Natas. 'I've shown them the true meaning of despair, and they want to walk out on me. Once you enter here you cannot leave.' His voice twisted with meanness.

'We're grateful for the extra company,' said Moloch,

'however briefly, before you all become shadows.'

'You foolish meddlers,' Fericul said darkly. 'Now you must sit in the shadow of real terror.'

'All love will ebb away from you in blackness and grief,' added Natas.

As they were speaking their evil words Vega noticed what looked like a star in the distance. It moved down the long passageway along the sheer edges, heading towards them, leaving a hem of rainbow colour behind.

There was a look of terror on Natas's face as he pointed to the strange light.

'What could it be?' asked Moloch.

'I don't know,' gasped Laab. 'But we must stop it. Magic Claw of Darkness, show your great power and destroy this—'

Before he could finish, Sacer entered, screaming through the darkness like a comet, enveloping all in a glorious light.

Laab was frozen with fear. They all looked at the swirling, dazzling colours showering down upon them. White, gold, rose pink, leaf green and bright orange splashed the walls, breaking the stranglehold of blackness, colours harmonising like music.

They could never have imagined such an abundance of light as they watched it dancing above them, diminishing the darkness. Pink arrows of radiance shot through Crag, Kos and Bawson. They could hear music in the lustre as it danced before their eyes. The sweetest of melodies, joyful trills, liquid notes rang in their ears.

The walls were gilded with yellow and crimson. Everything was illuminated. They could see points of light in the distance pricking the darkness.

Laab made a last attempt to summon the power of the Claw. With that, Sacer pulled the Sacred Feather from her wing and dropped it on Laab. There was an explosion of light. Shafts of colours coursed through the tunnels, enveloping all. The glorious hues streamed down like a waterfall. The most brilliant shades appeared again and again, pulsating, trans-forming, purifying. Purple, vermilion, vivid yel-lows, green, sky blue, white gold. The ground sparked as the light crashed down. Then, as it built up into great pillars of rainbow light, the chambers seemed unable to contain its power. The colours rose higher and higher until there was a sudden eruption of white light, followed by a loud crash. The light blasted outwards, its force shattering the place like glass.

Crag and the others could feel themselves being lifted up by the powerful force. Their hearts soared and they felt a boundless love as they were carried in the radiant light.

It released their minds from the bonds of grief. Crag could see Asrai trotting over a meadow with their family. Kos could see Noctua, Hoolet and Driad sitting in a tree on a beautiful moonlit night.

Tears flowed from Bawson as he watched the Straffan Clan rolling and playing in the silver light. They stopped and looked at him. They seemed so happy and contented.

Vega could see the tall mountain peaks and the clear blue skies. There, an eagle soared with his friends. It was Capella and the other birds from the falconry. Their wings were flying free at last. Sacer could see her parents circling and wheeling on sky-wings.

A beautiful feeling of warmth and love flowed into their hearts. They felt they were floating like leaves on the wind. Gently they seemed to drift down.

CHAPTER 23
Old Enemies

'I thought you were all lost,' remarked Sheila, standing over them as they lay on the river bank in the long grasses.

'How did we get here?' asked Hotchi.

'Search me,' said the heron. 'But you're all looking remarkably fit and well, despite your journey into Ratland.' And indeed they felt thoroughly invigorated and nourished after their contact with the mysterious light.

Crag sniffed the air. 'That feels wonderful, the cool touch of the wind on one's face.'

The black vulture stretched out his massive wings, aware of a great power and energy in them as he flapped. 'I have the wings of youth again, and it's all thanks to you,' he said, looking gratefully at Sacer.

'I feel the same,' said the bateleur eagle.

'Thank you for your selflessness and heroism.' Crag spoke tenderly to Sacer.

Sacer looked away towards a line of beech trees. In the distance a farmer was busy ploughing the stubble of his old grain crop. The chatter of magpies could be heard from an ash tree. Then, turning back slowly, Sacer looked into the sparkles of sunshine on the water and said sadly: 'I've lost the Sacred Feather.'

'You've destroyed the Claw of Darkness and the agents of death,' said Crag.

'And you've saved our skins,' said Hotchi.

'It was the power of the Sacred Feather, not I, dear friends,' said Sacer. 'And now I must away to the Sacred Cliffs and tell the ravens.'

'Would you like us to go with you?' asked Vega.

'No. I'd better go alone. I'll return though,' said Sacer, 'because I don't think the ravens will want me to remain at the Sacred Cliffs.' With those words she lifted her wings into the sky. Her friends called after her to take care as she sped away into the shallow sunlight, magpies calling in annoyance as she flew by.

Kos was anxious to leave and be reunited with his family. Crag and Bawson decided to say farewell to the other denizens of the wood before heading for their new home in the great forest. Kos said he would visit them soon.

* * *

When Kos arrived at the castle a harvest moon hung in the twilight. There were loud, shrill shrieks and hisses as Crannóg and Snowdrop called out to welcome him.

'You're a welcome sight,' said Kos to himself. Then with silent rapid wingbeats over the trees his family arrived to greet him. Hisses and snores of friendship were heard as they nudged and nuzzled him. A proud father had returned safely home.

* * *

Vega said he would journey later to the great forest, but that first he would visit his parents who were now on their second brood. 'It's been a good year for food. Lots of rodents around!'

Crag and Bawson watched him speed away like an arrow, his wounds all healed. They persuaded Hotchi to come and live in the great forest. 'By the time I get there I'll only be fit for hibernation,' he grumbled. 'It's all right for you old turtle doves.'

Barkwood, too, wanted to live in the great forest among the majestic trees, and hoped he could have many stimulating conversations with Hibou the wise one.

'Well, I'm content to patrol the rivers and canals around here,' said Sheila. 'There's not a lot for a heron to do in a forest, no matter how great it is. I must be away now. Do keep in touch, especially if there's any important information I should know. That is, if I haven't already heard it. Safe journey to Africa,' she said, looking at the vulture and the eagle.

'Thank you for all the times you came to visit us at the falconry,' the black vulture said to Sheila. 'You were our only link with the outside world.'

'Sorry it was mainly bad news I brought you,' she sighed. She raised her large wings, tucked in her neck and flapped away up river.

* * *

Sacer moved slowly in the chilly air. She really was in no hurry to return to the Sacred Cliffs, yet she must face the Council and report the loss of their most precious possession. It would be a terrible blow to them. Her eyes ever alert she noticed the ragged wingbeat of a crow in the distance, then the bird landed in a yew tree. It was a hooded crow. She passed, skirting low, checking the bird. It stared back. It wasn't Whizzer. She was relieved, yet prepared to fight if he should try to attack her again. Barkwood had warned her to be on the lookout for Whizzer. He felt the hooded crow would seek her out again.

Sacer was startled in her flight by a flurry of wings as twenty linnets came to mob her. She admired their brave little spirits so she quickened her wingbeats. They hung in the air, then descended to a hawthorn tree. The small birds seemed to sense that she was not hunting.

As she passed over a church steeple Sacer heard a harsh, guttural *kaah* cry. Whizzer seemed to swoop from nowhere. He hammered a swift blow to her back with his strong powerful beak. He had aimed for her head, which would have killed her instantly.

Sacer gave a loud scream. She weaved and dodged, swooping down in an effort to shake off her pursuer who was as determined as ever to finish her off. Cold and calculating, he had waited for this moment and was not about to let her escape now.

He chased Sacer, forcing her down. She skirted the ground then shot up into the air. From the safety of the hedges, startled robins and wrens watched the wild confusion of wings overhead, as the two enemies locked in savage combat. They somersaulted and tumbled in the air.

The hooded crow tried to get alongside the falcon. He didn't want to get ahead of her because he knew this would be dangerous. As he got closer he could plant a well-aimed hit at the eye. This would be enough to disable the peregrine, then he could strike a deadly blow to the head. They brushed alongside each other. Whizzer hammered a blow which missed the eye but hit the falcon's beak, causing a spurt of blood from her nostril.

Sacer kicked out and raked Whizzer's chest. The

hooded crow was wounded and faltered in mid-air. The peregrine rose upwards to gain height and line up her talons for the kill. She turned and dive-bombed the crow. A song thrush cowered in the field when he heard the electrifying scream of the attacking peregrine. A cloud of feathers burst into the air, and the hooded crow plummeted to the ground, having received a mortal blow.

A pheasant erupted from the stubble in a distant field. A stoat stood on its hindquarters and, having missed the cock pheasant, bounded over to the lifeless corpse of the crow, to claim it.

Sacer moved in wheeling circles across the sky, her heart still pounding. She called loudly in triumph. She was the supreme huntress.

* * *

The rolling clouds moved in, veiling the moon. For two days the lone Nusham had waited, determined to get the falcon that had killed his prize bird. Sleeping in the car was not much fun, especially since the wind had blown a gale, bringing driving rain with it. Still, he was determined to get the bird. Low clouds drifted over the face of the moon.

'More rain,' he growled. Hopefully the peregrine would show in the morning. He'd get some sleep and be back home before midday. He'd treat himself to a good breakfast in the Stag's Head after he'd killed the damn bird. 'Let's hope things go according to plan,' he muttered to himself as he tried to sleep.

*   *   *

Sacer came in low over the white-capped waves. She could see the unhurried flight of a gannet against the pale light. Moving at sea level, she flattened out above the waves, riding the blast that would take her to the base of the cliffs, which seemed quiet and deserted. As she came closer the current swept upwards, climbing the cliff face, and carried her up without much effort on her part. Flying along the edge of the cliffs, she alighted on a lichen-covered rock and scanned the surrounding area. Now that she was here, the realisation of what the loss of the Sacred Feather would mean to the ravens set her heart pounding again. Something gleamed up ahead beside the boulders. She suddenly became alert and attentive. The wooden pallets were new; she hadn't seen them before.

The man waited, tense, expectant. He'd seen her with his binoculars but she was still too far away to risk it. Sacer saw the glinting again beside the rock. She became anxious, bobbing her head then lifting off the ledge into the air. The man took aim, knowing he would have only one chance. His eyes never left the falcon. There was the thud of a gun and the clamour of gulls. A charge of shot spent. The falcon spiralled down.

The Nusham had hit his target. He quickly made his way down the dirt track, past the lighthouse and on to the car park. He knew there was a heavy penalty for shooting a protected species.

Sacer lay in a twisted heap below the ling heather.

CHAPTER 24

Ride the Wind

The foghorn boomed deep its triple warning from the lighthouse. Rachel looked out the window.

'The fog is lifting, Mum. I think I'll head up to Uncle Ned. I want to give him this feather. I'm sure it belongs to an owl.'

'You be careful and wrap up well,' said her mother from the kitchen. Mrs McCabe came out with some brown soda bread. 'Here. Bring this with you for him. And give him this as well,' taking a jar of jam from the cupboard. 'It's his favourite. Raspberry. Tell him to be sure and come for lunch on Sunday.'

She looked out the window. 'That fog is down for the day. You'd better take the torch. And change those shoes. Put on your hiking boots.'

'Mum, I'm sixteen, not a child. Oh, all right.' She plonked on the sofa and undid her shoes.

Her mother returned with the boots. 'They could do with a polishing.'

Rachel kissed her mother on the cheek and put on her coat.

'I'm off now, Mum,' she said. 'Oh, I nearly forgot the feather. I'd better bring Snaffles. Come on, girl.' The cocker spaniel hurried from her basket in the kitchen and wagged her tail furiously.

'No wet paws on your clothes,' said her mother.

'Mum, you should have been in the army – a sergeant ordering the troops about. No, more like a general.' Rachel stood to attention and saluted.

'Go on,' said her mother warmly. 'It's enough work managing you and your father.'

Rachel walked out over the fields. A robin sang its sad song from the gate post.

'Is your mate gone away again, cock robin?' she called to the little bird. The bird moved to the brambles and gave a *tick tick* call.

Rachel moved along the dirt track, stepping over large black slugs, then observed the glinting sparkle of spider webs across the gorse bushes. The spaniel sniffed the ground. The smell of rabbit was everywhere. The spaniel stopped suddenly and barked at the ground.

'Leave those rabbits alone,' yelled Rachel. The dog

barked again. 'What is it?' she asked as she moved over to the dog. 'My God!' she cried. 'A peregrine falcon!'

Sacer lay on her back, feebly holding her claws in defence.

'Oh, you poor thing,' said Rachel. A quick examination revealed blood smeared across the falcon's breast, and dull eyes. She gently lifted up the bird like a baby. A tear ran down her face. 'What cruel creep did this?' she snapped.

The falcon panted, sensing, however, no danger from this Nusham. Rachel tucked the bird inside her jacket, zipped it up and hurried to her uncle's house.

Uncle Ned was a man in his sixties, a retired lighthouse keeper. In his youth he had worked in many different jobs and had travelled a great deal.

At one time he'd been a falconer and used to buy and sell hawks and falcons. But he'd given all that up since his wife died. He'd gradually turned against the idea of owning such fine birds.

His house was still filled with pictures of birds, and with leather hoods and feathers he had collected over the years. A barn owl stared a frozen stare from under a glass dome. Two tawny owls were beautifully displayed in a large case, along with an original Lodge painting on the wall and several prints by Archibold Thorburn of goshawks and golden eagles.

'Is that you, Rachel?' Ned recognised her step. She

always came in the back door. Rachel burst in, tears streaming down her cheeks. 'What's the matter, honey?' He put his hands gently on her shoulders.

'Please, can you help, Uncle Ned?' she begged, blinking back the tears. She zipped down her jacket to reveal the injured bird.

'A peregrine falcon!' he exclaimed. Carefully he took the bird over to the table.

Rachel cleared off the miniature ship her uncle was making and switched on his desk light. He gave a sigh of deep regret as he examined the wounds on the bird.

'Hand me my glasses there, please, Rachel.' Putting them on, Ned carefully checked for anything broken. 'She's a lucky falcon. Probably lying on the headland all night. She's lucky she wasn't eaten by a fox or a mink. Even the magpies, if they'd discovered her would've made short work of her. There's some shot in the thigh and the breast. It damaged a lot of her primaries and secondaries too.'

Ned took a deep breath. 'I think we can help you, lady.'

Rachel broke into a broad smile and tears coursed down her face. She hugged her uncle.

'Why don't you go into the kitchen and make us a pot of tea,' Uncle Ned suggested.

'Mum sent some bread and jam,' Rachel interjected.

'Splendid.'

He went to his desk and took out a hood to cover

the falcon's eyes. Then he dosed her with tranquillisers. Using warm water, he washed the blood from her wounds. When the drugs took effect he removed the lead shot, then dusted the wounds with antibiotic powder.

After tea he took down a glass case, full of feathers. They were wrapped in plastic and neatly arranged by shape and size. There were primary feathers, secondary feathers and tail feathers, all collected over the years from moulting birds.

Rachel watched her uncle. He was like a surgeon preparing for an operation. Most of the peregrine's primaries were damaged. By trimming and shaping he would be able to restore the broken feathers. 'This is what's called imping.'

Rachel nodded wide-eyed.

'The feathers to be repaired are cut off at an angle, just below the break,' her uncle continued. 'Then replacement feathers the same size and shape as the severed ones are attached to the shaft.'

He placed a small wooden stick in the shaft of both feathers to make a link. When the feathers were fitted they were joined together and glued. The work was tedious and difficult. Rachel watched the concentration on his face. He carefully whittled the bamboo slivers which would join the broken shafts. Several hours and several cups of tea later he had replaced all the damaged feathers.

'You're a genius, Uncle Ned.' Rachel threw her arms around his neck.

'I'll leave her in the shed for the night,' Ned said. 'She'll be warm there. All things being equal she should be flying about in no time.' Then he added: 'Those feathers I replaced will do her until she moults them and grows a new set. Nature is wonderful,' he added and broke out into a broad smile.

* * *

Next day he drove to the nearest hatchery and got some dead day-old chicks for the falcon. He kept her for a fortnight.

'Well, it's time to release you, lady,' said Uncle Ned on a warm, sunny day. 'I'll give you the pleasure, Rachel.'

Rachel was wearing a pair of gardening gloves just in case the falcon might peck her, but that didn't happen.

'Away you go,' said Rachel as she cast the bird into the air. Sacer flapped, a little unsure of herself. But once she felt the wind under her she began to ride it.

'What a sight,' Uncle Ned said warmly. 'I think she'll be fine.'

'It's all thanks to you, Uncle,' said Rachel. 'By the way, I found this feather two weeks ago near the sand dunes. It looked like an owl's.' She pulled out the slightly bent feather.

He laughed. 'Yes, you're right. It is an owl's feather. Probably a short-eared owl. They come here in winter time.' The two of them, uncle and niece, strolled down the track near the cliffs. Rachel glanced over her shoulder and silently wished the falcon well.

*   *   *

Sacer heard the deep-throated *kronk-kronk* sounding over the cliffs and knew the ravens were near. She alighted on the plateau and looked about. Shimmer stood at the entrance to the cave, welcoming her. Corvus and Granet arrived out to greet her.

Sacer trembled and flew to them.

'We welcome your safe return, Sacer,' said Granet. 'You've done us proud. You've done your race proud. You may now take your rightful place as Guardian of the Sacred Cliffs. We'd be greatly honoured if you'd accept the title,' said Granet.

'And the challenge,' added Corvus warmly.

Sacer was about to tell them the terrible news of the loss of the Feather of Light, when to her horror she saw a rat coming out from the inner cave.

'Rats!' she cried in alarm, and was about to attack when Shimmer prevented her.

'Everything's all right,' said the rook reassuringly.

'We were just about to leave,' said a trembling Hack. Spike and Spook then appeared from inside the cave.

Granet, seeing the look of bewilderment in the

falcon's eyes, said calmly: 'I'd better explain. When you destroyed Ratland and its caverns of blackness you thought you'd destroyed the Sacred Feather in the process. But that was not so. These three rescued it and brought it back to us.'

'To make amends,' said Spook.

'After all we've done, we want to call a truce. There's no trickery involved,' insisted Hack. 'Now that the Claw of Darkness is destroyed along with Fericul, Natas, Moloch, Laab and the rest of those ghouls, we can all rest easy again.'

Sacer stood silently, greatly relieved that the Sacred Feather was back on the cliffs again.'

'We'll return to the city dump,' said Spook, 'and take our chances along with the other rodents and scavengers. Not that it's going to be easy when you stick out a mile like me with my lily-white fur. Still, I've survived before and hope to do so again.'

'Before you leave I want you to come inside once more. I have a gift for you three,' said Granet.

The rats twitched and looked puzzled. Inside, they stared once again at the beautiful feather with its golden light.

Granet said a few crow words over the feather, then lifting it up in his beak he touched each one of the rats in turn. They trembled, feeling a beautiful tingling sensation and a most exquisite peace. The feather had now returned to its original size. The other ravens helped Corvus place it back in its casket.

'Mmm, that felt so good!' said Spook. 'I feel as fit as a trout.'

'Look!' said Hack. 'Your fur is a rich chestnut-brown colour.'

'Well, that's a splendid gift. I thank you dearly,' said a very pleased Spook, as he licked his sleek fur.

'Can we still call you Spook?' asked Spike warmly.

'I'm well used to it. Your fang is gone, by the way!' he exclaimed to Spike.

Spike felt his mouth. 'I will be able to eat properly without cutting my lower lip. This is wonderful.'

'I see the improvement already,' said Hack. 'Every doe rat in the city dump will be tracking you now.'

Spook and Spike looked at Hack with open mouths. 'What is it?' he asked.

'Your eyes!' they exclaimed. Hack nervously put his claws to his eyes. He had two! He somersaulted about with glee. The ravens looked on, amused. The rats thanked them most graciously and scurried away down the slopes.

'You must be feeling hungry,' said Granet to Sacer. She nodded. 'We'll eat soon, but first there's someone I'd like you to meet.' Sacer watched one of the ravens glide away over the ridge, only to return in a few moments in the company of a very handsome tiercel. The male peregrine alighted near her. Sacer blinked her large eyes at him.

'He's escaped from the Nusham,' said the raven. Sacer could see the leather thongs around his legs. 'He's been wandering the cliffs hiding from them. We've given him sanctuary.'

'If the Council of Ravens welcome you on the Sacred Cliffs, then I, the last member of the guardians of the cliffs, also warmly welcome you,' said Sacer.

The tiercel looked tenderly at her and their eyes locked in contact. Then quickly turning away, Sacer said she must return to the lowlands again, as her friends would be anxious about her. There she would winter by the estuaries and seashore, and if it was all right with the elders she would return in springtime.

'This is now your home. You've done us proud. You're a credit to your clan,' said the raven.

'Hibou and his friends will be concerned about you, so I think we should head for the great forest,' said Shimmer, adding that by now Crag and the others would probably be living there.

'May I join you?' requested the male peregrine.

'We'd welcome your company,' said Shimmer. He looked at Sacer for approval, then in a teasing fashion she asked him if he wouldn't be afraid that the Nusham would get him. 'I'll take my chances,' he retorted, 'for the sake of your company.'

'Let's eat now,' said Corvus.

After they had eaten and regaled the elders with stories, it was time for the three of them to set out.

They said their farewells, took to their wings, and sped away.

*   *   *

In the ever-fading light, Regal the red deer watched from the forest as Shimmer and the falcons made their descent from the sky.

'Welcome, dear friends. It's good to see you return safely. Hibou is most anxious to hear all your news, in detail, of course. How are Crag, Bawson and the others?'

'They're safe and well,' said Sacer proudly. 'And I'm sure they're on their way here.'

'That will please Moonlight and Speedwell,' said the red deer, showing his amusement. 'Come,' he said warmly. 'Hibou and the others await you.'

CHAPTER 25

Winged Company

A hoot drifted faintly on the wing as Crag and his friends arrived at the edge of the great forest. The stars studded the chilly night sky. Amber eyes watched their arrival. Speedwell hurried out to greet them. Crag felt the gentle touch of the vixen as she brushed along his body and licked his face several times.

'Turtle dove,' teased Hotchi, trying to stifle a yawn.

Then they saw the great arched neck of the red deer behind a holly bush.

Regal came forward to greet them. 'It's with immense pleasure that we welcome your return,' he said.

They were led through the forest to the sunset tree. On the bough, the silhouette of the great owl could be seen as he sat motionless.

Hibou looked long and silently at them. 'It does my heart good to see you safely returned.' He gave a start when he saw the black vulture and the bateleur eagle among them.

Bawson explained how they had been prisoners for so very long and had now finally gained their freedom.

'This forest will always be a haven for wildfolk,' said Hibou. Then he cocked his head to listen. 'It's the whisper of wings,' he said softly, as the late migrants passed overhead. 'Second broods,' he chuckled.

'Is Kuick the nightjar still here?' asked Crag.

'He and his family left as the first leaves began to fall,' said Regal. Crag looked disappointed.

'There's no need to worry for us, dear friend,' said the black vulture. 'We feel confident of finding our way.'

'We can always follow the swallows and the martins,' said the bateleur.

Suddenly Bawson felt the velvet muzzle of Moonlight brush his face. 'Welcome back,' she whispered tenderly, then snuggled in tightly to him, lips and nostrils brushing over his face.

'More turtle doves,' sniggered Hotchi, trying to stifle a yawn. 'You'll forgive me, but I must rest. It's that time of year. Safe journey to Africa, big birds. Have a nice winter everyone. If you see Sacer give her my love.'

'Let me show you a suitable sleeping chamber,' said Regal.

'Oh, no need to go to any trouble. A pile of leaves will do nicely.' The deer pointed to a cosy, hollow trunk covered with mosses, with bracken at the entrance and a mound of leaves at the back. 'That's very suitable indeed, thank you, Noble, I mean, Regal. Good night. See you in springtime. Perhaps you could call me when the primroses are in bloom.'

*   *   *

The pale morning light saw the black vulture and the bateleur eagle swoosh away joyfully over the fields. The others watched their dark shapes winging away, Africa bound. Sacer was glad to have seen them before they left. As the tiercel watched the winged companions becoming specks in the distant sky, he too felt proud to think that mighty birds like those could get a second chance.

'You've learned much and shown great courage for one so young,' said Hibou to Sacer.

Sacer didn't feel so young anymore. 'I've learned that not all Nusham are enemies of the wildfolk,' she said.

'This is a good thing,' said the owl.

Bawson and Crag were amazed to learn that the rats had brought back the Sacred Feather.

'Rats,' growled Bawson.

'Well, love means that you forgive even when you can't forget,' said Barkwood.

'Is that from the *Sacred Book of Ravens*?' asked Shimmer.

'No. From *me*!' retorted Barkwood.

Regal whispered to Hibou, then looked at Crag and Bawson.

'I'd like some silence,' said the old owl, solemnly. The others looked on, a little puzzled. 'By the powers of the forest I declare that Speedwell and Crag, Moonlight and Bawson should become mates,' he declared. There were loud cheers of approval from the rest.

A great excitement bubbled up inside Bawson. He looked at Moonlight, her warm eyes gazing back at him. 'Nothing like this has ever happened to me before,' he blurted out. Then he gingerly nuzzled her.

'Well after all,' added Hibou, 'among us wildfolk it's the female who chooses her mate.'

Crag sat crouched and contented, Speedwell in front of him, her inviting eyes filled with light.

The old owl then turned to Sacer and the tiercel. 'What about you two?' he asked.

Sacer looked softly at the tiercel, then back to the owl. 'I'd better not rush into any close bonding just yet,' she said. Then in a teasing tone she added: 'Besides, I don't even know his name.'

'Falco,' he replied, intimately.

Then, a little embarrassed, Sacer said: 'Let's not waste this fine morning when we could be exploring the estuary.' She opened her wings and sped away, Falco darting after her.

'Be back by evening glow. We have a lot to talk about,' boomed the old owl. 'Barkwood, I was just thinking. You should live above me in the sunset tree.'

'That would be an honour,' replied Barkwood.

'Well, I must be away myself,' said Shimmer. He promised to keep in touch, then, after saying his farewells, he headed off to the rookery.

Moonlight and Speedwell decided to show their new mates the forest. 'Come with us to the quiet forest where no Nusham goes,' Moonlight whispered to Bawson in loving tones.

Bawson laughed a giddy laugh.

'You old turtle dove,' said Crag to him as they padded away.

'You're one to talk,' smiled Bawson as they padded away.

CHAPTER 26

Sky Wings

Blustery March winds sweep through the heather. Gorse flowers splash their yellow abundance on their prickly bushes, celebrating spring's arrival. The yellowhammer constructs its cup-shaped nest within the prickly haven of the bush. The guillemots and gulls are on their breeding ledges on the fearful cliffs, which fall hundreds of feet to the sea. Cormorants fly low above the heaving waves.

The fresh morning echoes with the cries of the peregrines. Rachel and her uncle stand by the gateway of the farm watching the spectacle, as the graceful birds soar and twist in the watery skies.

'Those birds are the very spirit of this place,' says Uncle Ned.

'Do you think perhaps one of these could be the

bird we rescued?' Rachel asks her uncle, linking him by the arm.

'It's hard to say, really. Yet there aren't too many of their kind around here.'

'I just *know* one of them is our bird,' she says.

'I didn't know you were psychic,' her uncle teases in mocking tones. 'Or can you see the feathers I put in?'

'Yes, I can especially see the second one from the left. That's definitely your handiwork!'

Her uncle laughs warmly as they head down the dirt track.

Sacer hangs motionless in the air, watching the two Nusham leave the area. Her mate rides the wind. She quickly planes down along the cliff face after him. Falco is glad that he's finally rid himself of the leather jesses. Now he can feel truly free. He has left all but memories of the falconry behind him. Now he has a home, and an exceedingly beautiful mate. Sacer looks back at him tenderly.

'Follow me,' she cries, as she heads over the plateau.

The ravens watch from the rocks. Granet says proudly: 'We now have our guardians of the Sacred Cliffs.'

OTHER BOOKS IN THE *WINGS* WILDLIFE FANTASY TRILOGY

ON SILENT WINGS

An orphaned barn owl fights for his own and the world's survival against the evil rat Fericul.

Paperback £4.99/€6.34/$7.95

WILD WINGS

Vega, a kestrel, escapes from a falconry, but the world is under threat from a gang of rats who have escaped from a laboratory. Can Vega help save the world from darkness?

Paperback £4.99/€6.34/$7.95

ALSO BY DON CONROY

CARTOON FUN

Draw your own cartoons and get excellent results – people, animals, faces, comic strips, super heroes, monsters, dinosaurs, birds. Easy-to-follow instructions and great fun. It *really* works!

Paperback £4.99/€6.34/$7.95

WILDLIFE FUN

How to create lively and true-to-life drawings as well as cartoon animals. Fail-safe instructions and models to follow. Includes lots of information on the lives of the animals. Full of fascinating fun.

Paperback £4.99/€6.34/$7.95

Send for our full-colour catalogue